THE GREAT AND TERRIBLE QUEST

by

Margaret Lovett

Originally published in 1967 by Holt, Rinehart and Winston. Permission to reprint this book was sought from Holt, Rinehart and Winston and all known subsidiaries and assigns. Current copyright owner is unknown.

This edition published 2007 by Avyx, Inc.

Avyx, Inc.
8032 South Grant Way
Littleton, CO 80122-2705
USA
(303) 483-0140

www.avyx.com

ISBN 978-1-887840-32-3
ISBN 1-887840-32-X

THE GREAT AND TERRIBLE QUEST

Chapter One

TRAD found the white-haired stranger by nearly putting an arrow into him, thinking he was a rabbit. Trad's wicked old grandfather, who liked people to believe he was a wizard, had gone out very early and would not be back until dark. This was the very first time Grandfather had gone away from the hut for more than an hour or two without leaving someone in charge of the boy, and he had left many tasks to keep Trad busy, but since the boy had come to live with him six years ago, when he was only four, he had learned to pretend to be much slower and stupider than he really was. He had finished all the work while the sun was still high in the sky and had come out on to the wild moorland behind their stone hut with the little three-legged half-starved dog he had managed to hide from his grandfather for nearly a month. Usually they shared the stale loaf and moldy lump of cheese which was Trad's daily ration, but today the boy had promised the dog and himself a feast of rabbit.

The little dog had pounced on one as soon as they were right out on the wildest part of the moor, which was too far for him to come by himself even if Trad had thought it safe to let him wander about on his own. Though he brought it at once to Trad, the boy had let him eat the whole of it, meaning to get one for himself and perhaps a couple more for the next day or two, though they would not keep for long in this hot weather.

A few minutes later he saw a flash of white behind a bush and quickly drew his bow, but luckily waited for a moment before shooting, for in that moment it became obvious that whatever was moving behind the bush was very much larger than a rabbit.

He dropped down flat in the knee-high heather and peered through the wiry stems, watching with astonishment as a grown man with a shock of short white hair all over his face crawled slowly on his hands and knees from the other side of the bush. Outlaws and madmen both lurked in this wild moorland and Trad lay very still, keeping one hand over the little dog's muzzle, though the animal, used to danger, was lying there still and silent. Then, holding his breath and wriggling noiselessly, Trad began to move backwards, when unexpectedly the crawling man gave a loud groan and crashed down on his face.

Nothing in Trad's short and difficult life had yet managed to teach him not to rush to the help of anyone in trouble, and without stopping to think he left his shelter and ran to the man's side. Since he lay without movement the boy turned the heavy head towards him and saw through the tangle of white hair a face which was nearly as white, and lips that were cracked with thirst.

He had a little water with him in a leather bottle his grandfather had once thrown away, and he trickled this carefully into the man's mouth. A deep sigh followed the first painful gulping, and then the man began to struggle up. Trad helped him with all his small strength, and when the stranger was sitting up he knelt before him, offering the last hard crust of his loaf.

The man put his hand out quickly and then stopped.

"Have you eaten?" said a deep husky voice.

"Yes," said Trad, thinking stoutly about the half loaf he had eaten first thing that morning, and with another sigh the man accepted the bread and ate it slowly and neatly. Then at last he began to turn his head and look about him.

"Where—where is this?" he asked hesitantly.

Trad was puzzled how to answer him. As far as he knew, this place had no name, it was just the moor, and his grandfather's hut was the only building within miles.

"I live over there," he said doubtfully, waving one dirty hand in the direction he had come. "There is no town or village. And the City—" he pronounced the word carefully because he had only heard it once or twice and barely knew what it meant "—is many, many days' journey to the north."

"The City!"

The stranger's red-rimmed eyes suddenly opened widely, blazing brilliantly blue, but the next moment they were dull and blank.

"I have forgotten, I have forgotten," he muttered, putting his hand up to his head.

Trad looked at him pitifully. Somehow this old man reminded him of the little three-legged dog when he had first seen him panting his life away under a thorn bush.

As if the thought of the dog had called him, the animal was suddenly there, licking first Trad's hand and then the hand of the stranger.

"Jokey likes you!" exclaimed Trad joyfully.

"Jokey?" repeated the deep voice vaguely.

"I call him Jokey because he always looks as if he's laughing," explained Trad. "What's your name?"

There was an odd silence. The man was staring at him blankly.

"I have forgotten," he said at last in the same toneless mutter, and when Trad asked him where he had come from and where he was going to he only shook his head helplessly, saying the same thing over and over.

Trad asked no more questions but began to consider what to do. He could probably hide the man in the rock tunnel where Jokey had been lying for the past month, but whether three of them could live on one person's food—he shrugged his shoulders. That could be settled when the time came, the first thing was to get the old man into shelter before Grandfather got back.

"Come with me," he said. "I'll look after you."

He wondered in a worried way if the man could walk, because he was much too big for Trad to drag him, but although he needed a little help to get up, once he was on his feet he walked steadily enough in the direction Trad led him, while the boy carried Jokey.

The hiding place was some distance away. Grandfather's solitary stone hut was built up against a great rock, in fact the rock itself was the back wall of the building and hid it from the roadway, or rather track, that ran north and south across the moor. The tunnel ran between some smaller rocks jumbled a bowshot away. Trad had crawled into it hoping that it led to a cave, but although the crack was about twenty feet long, it was nowhere much higher or wider than three feet, and at the end it narrowed down to a rabbit hole. However, it took a sharp turn just after the entrance so that it made a good hiding place for anyone lying flat, and Trad explained anxiously to the man that he could come out to stretch when it was dark, and that he himself would bring him food and water. He was not quite sure how much the man understood of what was said to him, so he repeated very earnestly, "Please, you will promise not to come out in the daylight, it would be dangerous."

The white head nodded once.

"You have my knightly word," said the deep voice matter-of-factly, and the man got down on his hands and knees again and crawled very carefully into the hole.

Trad watched him with his eyes and even his mouth wide open. A *knight*! This old half-starved wanderer was a *knight*! Of course he might be a madman who thought he was a knight—but even as this came into his mind the boy realized that from the beginning he had been puzzled by the stranger's voice. He sounded like Grandfather and Grandfather's friends, and though Trad hated and feared his grandfather and disliked nearly all his friends he had always been attracted by the smoothness and quietness of their voices, so different from the harsh rough bellowing of the country people he occasionally saw when they brought supplies.

Trad shut his mouth with sudden determination.

The old man had been in enough danger from Grandfather even as an ordinary beggar or peasant; if he really was a knight the danger was deadly, and Trad made up his mind to save him whatever happened. He glanced at the sky. He would just have time to fill the bottle with water again to leave with the man tonight, and then he must get back to make sure everything was ready for the guests Grandfather would have later.

Something touched his ankle. Startled, he looked down to see Jokey sitting there, grinning all over his face, with another dead rabbit at his feet.

"Oh clever, clever boy!" said Trad softly.

Squatting down he divided the rabbit in half with his old blunt knife, gave the front half to Jokey and tucked the roughly skinned back half into his belt. He would slip it into the caldron in which supper was cooking, and bring it with him in the early morning when Grandfather was asleep. He ran quickly to the spring, filled the leather bottle and came back to the tunnel, crawling carefully on top of the man's legs until he could put the bottle in his hand.

"Can you reach to drink?" he asked.

The man had turned on his back and was lying in the widest part of the tunnel, so that by moving slowly he could bring his hand up to his mouth.

"Thank you, yes. Thank you for all your care," he murmured, and the careful courtesy when he was so obviously exhausted made Trad even more sure that he was indeed a knight.

"I will be back in the morning," he promised, and wriggled backwards out into the open.

Jokey, who had learned very quickly that he must hide himself whenever Trad was not there, limped at once into the hole with all that was left of the rabbit in his mouth, and Trad heard him gnawing away just out of sight around the corner.

All this had taken longer than he had reckoned, and he only just had time to hide his bow and arrows and get into the kitchen before he heard the faint sounds of Grandfather arriving. The old man always came quietly, as if he expected to catch Trad in mischief, but it was so long since this had happened that it was really only a habit now, and Trad could take a moment to pop his half-rabbit into the caldron, rub his sticky hands in the ashes, and use the bellows on the fire which was still burning steadily through the thick logs he had piled on before he went out.

"H'm," said Grandfather, clouting the boy across the head in his usual greeting. "Stir your lazy bones and get supper ready—four guests will be arriving within the hour."

Trad picked himself out of the ashes and began to scurry in a bewildered way about the room. Slowness and stupidity got him many beatings, but because Grandfather believed he had succeeded in turning the bright gay little boy who had come to him into a cowed half-wit, he occasionally left him alone or gave him time to himself, and Trad counted that worth all the beatings. In his various stumblings from cupboard to table he sneaked a wooden bowl into the dark corner of the fireplace, and when the table was laid and the trampling of horses outside drew Grandfather to the doorway, he coolly ladled out his bit of rabbit together with a few vegetables and filled the hidden bowl.

He was only just in time, for Grandfather turned sharply and gave him an unusually close look. Trad hung his mouth open a bit further and shuffled his bare feet. While working he had pushed his tangle of hair off his forehead, and now Grandfather's heavy hand swept it back right over his face.

"Keep it like that," he said dangerously. "Who wants to see that stupid look? Go out and tether the horses, then come back and serve the food. And wash your hands—these are gentlemen."

This was something new. Most of Grandfather's friends were or had been gentlemen, but they had been a robber band for so long that little things like dirty hands no longer bothered them—they sat down at table sometimes without wiping the blood from their own hands. Alert and curious, Trad stepped outside. He was used to handling horses even in the semidarkness and liked it best of all his tasks, but tonight he did not linger with them and on the pretext of finding it difficult, he came straight back.

He had dipped his hands in the trough ready-filled there for the horses and wiped them on the seat of his ragged breeches, but even so Grandfather for once took over the job of ladling the rich stew into the wooden bowls.

"Eat, my lord, though the food is unworthy," he said ceremonially, and Trad peeped through his hair at the man so unusually addressed. He was plainly, even shabbily dressed, but he wore a great ruby ring on one finger, and in the light of the thick wax candle on the table his dark harsh face showed arrogant with the knowledge of high birth and importance.

Trad, who had learned all he knew of the world by listening to Grandfather's guests, listened even more carefully than usual. With the man addressed as "my lord" was another stranger, so respectful that Trad thought he must be a servant, and two of Grandfather's usual friends, of whom the soft-spoken one who called himself Diamond and was the cruelest of the lot was speaking to the strange lord without noticeable courtesy.

"Well, we did your job for you. Tonight you pay over the money as agreed."

"I should have liked to have seen the man's dead

body," said the lord coldly. "You are sure he is dead?"

Diamond laughed.

"No man could have lived with such a wound in his head. And three of my men are dead and two more disabled—that must be reckoned in our pay."

"I warned you to take plenty of men," snapped the stranger.

Diamond's fist hit the table, making the candle flame flicker and then flare wildly.

"I had fifteen men—fifteen proved fighters to one. And I myself only live because Bron here crept up behind him and smote him with his great axe. Who was this man—this champion of champions?"

The lord did not answer. He was staring at Trad, shown up clearly for a moment by the sudden brilliant light.

"Who is this boy?" he said sharply.

Grandfather leaned forward.

"My grandson. Alas—" he heaved a great sigh "—a poor half-wit! My daughter, my only child, chose to run away from me with a beggar who came playing a lute—a lord, no less, she said he was." Grandfather's lip curled into his most contemptuous expression. "And when she and the beggar both lay dead of the plague I took their brat out of the gutter from the goodness of my heart."

Diamond laughed mockingly.

"Well, it saves paying a servant, and the boy is too stupid to betray you."

Grandfather's eyes glinted angrily, but he never quarreled with Diamond.

"As you say," he said smoothly. "Look at him, my lord—is he a danger to anyone?"

They all looked at Trad, who hung his head, whimpered a little, and let tears trickle out of his eyes and some dribble from his mouth. This was a trick he had learned early on, and it always worked. All the men laughed, cruelly or scornfully, and forgot him at once. He scuttled into a corner like a little animal and crouched there. What Grandfather had just said was more than he had ever learned about himself, and he was so busy thinking about it that he missed the next bit of talking.

His mother had thought his father was a *lord*—was *he* a lord, then? And the broken lute he had rescued from the rubbish corner and carefully restrung must have been his father's. He could hardly remember the father and mother who had died together of the plague, but against all his grandfather's contemptuous references to beggars and half-wits he had kept a bright clear picture in his mind of a little garden with flowers in it and three people laughing, himself and two grown-ups whose faces were a blur but whose arms were around him lovingly. It was this picture more than anything which had saved him from becoming the frightened imbecile his grandfather thought him, and as he considered the words Grandfather had said, the picture seemed to grow brighter and clearer.

He drew a long unsteady breath, and then because experience had taught him to keep his wits alert while Grandfather was about, he put away the thoughts for a time when he would be alone and began to listen again to the men at the table.

The strange lord was leaning forward, staring accusingly at Grandfather.

"You failed in *your* search, for all your fine words," he was saying harshly. "Six years ago you told me you could find him, and since then I have had nothing but excuses."

"My lord, I fear it is true." Grandfather's voice was smooth and regretful, but as Trad peeped at him his interest sharpened. The old man's eyelids were half over his eyes, hooding them like a vulture, and Trad had learned that this happened when Grandfather was lying. "But all the clues were so vague, so uncertain. A man of twenty-five or more—thirty or more now—with 'silver hidden in the gold'—no, I found no trace of him." He laughed a little. "But at least, my Lord Regent, you need not now fear that he will ever be found by your laughing lord."

"Thanks to me and my men," put in Diamond, his voice soft and dangerous. "Three months, my lord, three months, and we are still waiting for payment. We at least did not fail."

The lord turned to look at him arrogantly.

"So you say," he snapped. "How do I know you even found him, let alone left him dead?"

Trad, who had come to know Diamond well, thought that a very sensible suspicion, and though the man himself scowled he did not waste time in claiming to be honest. He put a hand into his wallet and then threw something on to the table.

"We found that on a chain around his neck under his armor. Maybe you recognize it?"

The harsh dark face showed an instant's complete stupefaction. Then the man put out his hand, but Grandfather got there first. Swooping down, his long rather dirty fingers picked up the little object and held it into the light of the candle.

"Ah!" he said. "A ring of gold. With a thin thread of silver on the *inside*—" his gaze swung round. "Is *this* what you meant by 'silver hidden in the gold'?"

He sounded angry and disbelieving, but he was nothing like as angry as the lord, who sprang to his feet with a sharp curse and snatched the ring so suddenly that Grandfather was taken by surprise and let it go.

"None of your business. None of your business," snarled the dark man, as with shaking fingers he fumbled at the fastening of his pouch.

Grandfather, veiling the fury in his eyes with his heavy eyelids, was snapping his fingers softly.

"A ring—a ring—but only the half of a ring, I think —I have seen these trick rings, one snaps around the other and the two become one—" he muttered, but broke off suddenly as the stranger leaned forward and struck him viciously across the face.

"I said that it was none of your business." The usually harsh voice was softer and even more dangerous than Diamond's. "You have had your uses, old man, and been repaid with our protection. If you became—a nuisance—we could leave you to the Law."

Grandfather sat very still. Even in the uncertain flickering light the red mark of the blow showed angry against his white beard. Trad, sheltering behind his up-lifted arms in case Grandfather's look should light on him and realize that he had seen the blow, caught a glimmer of an amused smile on Diamond's face, but he himself felt nothing but terror at the thought of what Grandfather might do. He did not really believe in the magical powers of which the old man boasted, for he had had to help with too many tricks which were supposed to be magic, but he knew only too well the power of his wickedness and malice. He cared little for the life of this strange and unpleasant lord, but if Grandfather killed him and had to flee he would take Trad with him, and then who would look after the poor old man and the little dog hidden in the tunnel?

But Grandfather, after sitting like stone while Trad's heart thumped perhaps twenty times, bent his head almost humbly.

"An old man's wits, like those of children, dart here and there without meaning harm," he murmured. "Forgive me, my Lord Regent, the ring is forgotten. Do not take your protection from me."

The lord's lip curled in a sneer, and he did not even take the trouble to answer. He turned away from the table, saying over his shoulder, "Pay them what is owing, and let us leave this hovel."

A heavy bag was flung on the table and Diamond seized it greedily, spilling gold coins on to the table and counting them with practiced speed. Trad, who was used to seeing the rewards of robberies and deeds of violence counted there on the table, opened his eyes wider in astonishment. From the enormous price being paid, the killing of that one man must have had some extraordinary value to this Lord Regent.

Diamond looked up from his neat piles.

"Generous, my lord," he purred. "I hope you have other enemies." He laughed evilly and slid one of the bigger piles across the table to Grandfather. "Your share, Master Wizard," he said with smooth mockery.

Grandfather's eyes were still veiled. Without a word he put out his hand and dropped the coins, uncounted, into his pouch. Then his head turned towards the corner where Trad crouched.

With the animal instinct of the ill-treated, the boy had one moment before huddled further into the corner, closed his eyes and opened his mouth. It would be much better if Grandfather believed he had been asleep all this time.

Diamond's look had followed the old man's.

"No danger indeed," he laughed, and swept the gold back into the leather bag. Then he swung around on his stool and aimed a shrewd kick at the child.

Trad yelped as his head hit the wall—he remembered dimly being taught not to cry out when he was hurt, but he had learned quite quickly that courage brought further punishment and now he yelled or wept just enough to satisfy them—and stumbled up. Knuckling his eyes and snuffling a little he listened to the sharp order to see the guests out. The preparation of a torch of pine wood and pitch had been one of his tasks earlier that day, and he lit it at the glowing fire, then led the way out to the horses.

He did not expect anyone to speak to him, but as

Diamond and Bron got the horses ready for the strangers, he was startled to hear the lord's harsh voice in his ear.

"Listen, boy. Are you dumb as well as half-witted?"

"N-n-no, master," he stuttered.

"Then hear me. I will give you a silver piece. Next time my servant comes this way you will tell him of *any* visitors your grandfather has had. Do you understand?"

Trad could see the danger of showing that he was not as stupid as supposed, though he longed for that silver piece. With it he might even dare to run away from Grandfather. He began to snuffle again.

"I dursn't," he mumbled in the thick country dialect. "Granfer'd beat me to death."

There was an angry exclamation in the gloom.

"Give him two coins, Perrault," snapped the lord. "Two more, boy, when you tell him of your grandfather's visitors. And the old man shall never know. Keep your eyes open especially for a tall slim man with golden hair."

The last words were hissed into his ear after Diamond had shouted that all was ready, and without another look the lord strode off. The man he had called Perrault paused only for a moment to fumble for the boy's hand and press two large coins into it, then he hurried after his master.

Trad was shaking with excitement but he steadied himself to hold the torch high while the men mounted and rode off. He didn't have to think about hiding the money from Grandfather, and he had already decided what to do with it. As soon as the sound of hoofs was small in the distance he plunged the torch into a patch of mud, and as the light died spluttering he pushed the coins between the tightly bound pine branches until he could no longer feel them, put the dead torch carefully under the water trough where it was hidden, and went back to the hut. He had to brace himself before going through the door because he knew what sort of mood his grandfather would be in, and indeed the beating he got was the worst he ever remembered. But as he crawled whimpering into the dark corner furthest from the fire, that bright picture of laughing love and the thought of the two hidden coins gave him comfort stronger than he had known for a long time, and he fell asleep quite quickly in spite of his throbbing back.

Chapter Two

A KICK and a curse from Grandfather which opened his eyes to the dim dawn light reminded him that he had meant to wake early to take the bowl of food out to the tunnel, but then he had expected Grandfather to sleep late after his visitors. He crept out unsteadily, so stiff and aching that the tears in his eyes were genuine, and as he stood upright he saw with surprise that Grandfather was again dressed for traveling. He had never known this to happen two days running, and his heart leaped at the thought of another day's freedom. He might even—the memory of the two coins outside made him suddenly dizzy with hope—be able to run away far enough for Grandfather not to catch him.

He kept his head down and his eyes looking at the floor in case Grandfather should see them and be able to read his thoughts, and it was because of this that he saw the tiny gleam of gold among the rushes on the floor. He had cleared out the dirty rushes and put down clean ones only yesterday, so that the layer was not as thick as usual, but it had been thick enough to muffle the sound of whatever had fallen last night. His first thought was that it must be one of Diamond's gold coins, but as he instinctively moved forward so that one of his bare feet covered the betraying gleam he felt even through the tough sole a circle both sharper and smaller than those coins had been. The ring? Could it be the ring which had so startled the strange lord and got Grandfather that blow across the face? He remembered how the lord's fingers had been shaking as he put the ring away—perhaps he had fumbled it and not heard the tiny sound of the fall because he was listening to Grandfather's mutterings about the other half of the ring.

Trad's mind worked fast. In that case either the lord or his servant was likely to be back as soon as the loss was discovered, and if Grandfather was not here——

To his surprise he found himself even more afraid of the Lord Regent than he was of Grandfather. That settled it. It was today he must run away, as soon as Grandfather left, taking Jokey and the old man with him.

He had been listening with half an ear to Grandfather's harsh instructions. Enough work to keep him busy for three days was being piled on him, but he need not now burden his memory with that. His usual ration of bread and cheese was not given to him, he was to be allowed to scrape out last night's stew— "and if I am not back tonight it will do you no harm to go hungry until the peasants bring next week's food," said Grandfather grimly. "If any come inquiring for me—"

he hesitated, then gave a sharp bark of laughter "—you are to tell them I have gone to see to the affairs of a dead friend."

"A dead friend," repeated Trad stupidly and got a cuff across the head which knocked him down. He managed to crumple up where he had been standing, hugging himself in a snuffling ball right on top of the little circle of gold, and Grandfather only gave him a contemptous kick as he strode past, warning him that all the work must be done by the time he returned, or last night's beating would seem like a mother's spanking.

"My mother never spanked me," whispered Trad into the crook of his arm as he heard the old man's boots ring on the stone threshold Trad himself laboriously scrubbed day by day, and as soon as the sound of the footsteps died away he scrambled up. It would be like Grandfather to creep back to spy on him, so after a quick glance to make sure that the gold was hidden, he went straight to the caldron of stew.

There was more in it than he had expected, and with the bowlful he had put aside the night before, the three of them would have a larger meal than either he or Jokey were accustomed to, or the old knight either, judging by his gaunt looks and sharp bones. Trad eyed wistfully the locked cupboard in which the food was kept, but he was desperate to be away before anyone from the Lord Regent came, and it would take time to break open the door. He scraped the caldron clean into the hidden bowl, which was now brimming full, then ran to the door and saw that Grandfather was not going to come back this time, he was already hardly visible along the rough track which led north.

"We'll go south," decided Trad at once, and scrabbled in the rushes for the hidden gold.

It was indeed a ring, and looking at it carefully in the growing light he saw the thin thread of silver which Grandfather had described on the inside. The bowl was going to take two hands to carry without spilling, so after a moment's thought he put the ring in his mouth and, when he got outside, rescued the two silver coins and put them in the same safe place.

In spite of his fear he did not go straight to the tunnel. He had another nook among the rocks, not big enough for a person, where he kept his bow and arrows and the mended lute which he had loved even without knowing that it was his father's. He had thought of a possible hiding place for the ring, which he realized was a terribly dangerous possession, and after he had put the bowl very carefully on a level place, he pulled the lute out.

It was a beautiful instrument, inlaid with ivory and gilt, and as he remembered, a circle of ivory had begun to come away from one of the rosettes, leaving only the gilt center.

Scraping with his dirty broken nails he got the rest of the ivory out and in growing excitement laid the gold ring in its place. It fitted as if the circle had been made for it, and when he pressed hard the ring sank down into the wood with a sharp click. Only the edge of it showed, and that blended so perfectly with the gilt of the center of the rosette that it might have been part of it.

The extraordinary good luck of this made Trad suddenly shiningly happy and sure that everything would go well. He tied the coins into a corner of his filthy ragged shirt, quickly slung his bow over one shoulder and the lute over the other, picked up the bowl again and hurried off to the tunnel. He bent down, calling out, "Come out, sir, it's quite safe."

Jokey popped out first, bouncing silently on his three paws all around Trad, and then the man's legs appeared, jerking as he worked himself with some difficulty around the sharp bend. He gave a sigh of relief when he could straighten out and climb to his feet.

Trad went down on one knee as in his dreams a page did to a lord and offered the brimming bowl of stew. Gravely the white-haired man took it from him and then surprised the boy by producing from somewhere among his rags a horn spoon.

"Come, child," said the deep soft voice. "Will you eat first or shall I?"

"I'll have what you leave," said Trad at once, thinking that then he would be able to give Jokey some in the bowl, however little he had himself. But the bowl was handed back to him more than half full, and when he put it down with a generous share for the little dog he himself felt comfortably fed.

As he bent down, the cord of the lute rubbed through the holes in his shirt against his sore back, and he caught his breath at the sharp pain. The next moment a strong arm was around him and firm gentle hands pulled his shirt up to show his back. At the sight of the old scars and the new bruises and cuts the white-haired man let go of him slowly.

"Alas! Alas! The sorrow of the world!" said the deep voice brokenly, and as Trad peeped around he saw that the man was weeping, the large tears streaming down in a flood of pure pity.

Trad, who had only known tears of fear or pain or deceit, was deeply impressed. He was going to comfort the man by explaining how used he was to beatings when he happened to see Jokey, who had stopped trying to lick the last taste of the gravy from the bowl and was staring towards the north, both black ears pricked.

Trad's first fear was that Grandfather was coming back, but his quick hearing, nearly as tuned to danger signals as Jokey's, soon caught the regular beat of hoofs.

"The Lord Regent!" he gasped. "Hide, sir, hide!"

"The Lord Regent!"

For a moment Trad was startled again by the brilliant blue of the stranger's eyes as he stood, tall and alert, looking at the boy, but then the straight figure crumpled and the eyes dulled.

"I have forgotten—I have forgotten," he groaned.

"You will remember, you *will,*" said Trad in a passion of comfort. "But now please please hide, this is danger."

Obediently the man turned and crawled back into the tunnel, drawing up his legs as far as he could to leave room for Trad and Jokey. The little dog followed him, but the boy had been thinking fast. Of them all he was in least danger, and he wanted intensely to know what was going on. He hastily took off the lute and bow and stuffed them out of sight in the tunnel, but he himself lay down behind a tall rock and peered cautiously around it.

He did not have long to wait. The mounted party which rode into sight was traveling fast and soon reached the hut. There they halted, and as they got off their horses Trad could see that the Lord Regent was not with them though his servant Perrault was. It was too far away to hear what he was saying, but he was obviously giving sharp orders and the tough-looking soldiers jumped to obey. They went into the hut but came out almost at once, and after another sharp order spread out into a search party. Trad ducked behind his rock, his heart bumping, but they did not come far. When a long silence made him risk peeping out again he could see no one but the one soldier guarding the horses, but out of the open door of the hut came flying pots and pans, firewood, stools, the rushes from the floor and then, broken in pieces, Grandfather's great carved and painted wooden bedstead. They were searching for the ring, Trad knew, and he laughed silently in high delight as he thought where it was.

Time passed, a time which seemed endless to the watcher and then Perrault came out followed by the soldiers. It could be seen that he was in a filthy temper, and one of the soldiers approached him very cautiously. He was struck across the face but persisted, and at last Perrault listened to him as he waved his arm towards the north and then pointed to the sun. He was saying, Trad thought alertly, that Grandfather would have traveled to the north with the ring, and with the sun still low in the sky could not have gone far. Perrault seemed to be convinced, for he barked another order and with great speed the whole party mounted and rode off the way they had come.

Giving them just time to get out of sight Trad wriggled back to the tunnel, called a warning to stay hidden for a little, and himself ran at top speed to the hut.

The place was a shambles, with cupboards broken open and all Grandfather's possessions flung about. The boy did not waste time looking for money, for he knew quite well Grandfather never kept any in the hut, he had a secret hiding place somewhere else for anything valuable, but with food they could travel a long way before having to show themselves and so perhaps Grandfather would not be able to follow them. The soldiers seemed to have taken pleasure in spoiling everything they touched, but Trad had never had enough food to know that dirt was supposed to make it uneatable. He scraped some stamped-on cheeses and broken loaves into an old sack, added a flask of wine which had been hidden under one of the hearthstones and which the soldiers had missed, and hauled the lot triumphantly to the tunnel.

Rescuing the bow and lute first, he called the man and Jokey out. He was just going to say that they could run away together now, when the stranger got in first.

"You spoke of danger, child," he said crisply, as a soldier might speak. "What is this danger?"

Trad wrinkled his forehead. The danger from the

Lord Regent he hardly understood himself, and in any case he could not explain it without mentioning the ring, which he was afraid to do, so important did it seem to be. But the danger from Grandfather was just as great, and that was easy to explain.

"No stranger who comes here is allowed to live," he said. The horror with which he had first understood this had become dulled by time, though he had never come to take it for granted. Jokey and this man were not the first he had warned or hidden, but there had been several he had not been able to save, and his eyes darkened at the thought of them. "This is the place where a band of robbers come to get their orders or their pay. My—" he stopped suddenly and went crimson. He had never had to say this to anyone before, and he could hardly make himself do it. "My grandfather is the one who gives the orders and arranges the pay," he whispered. "I don't know who he gets them from, but I think perhaps anyone who wants an enemy killed or a house burned down or someone beaten up."

"Alas, alas, the sorrow of the world," murmured his hearer and again large clear tears flowed down the thin cheeks.

Trad waited respectfully, but his mind was working hard.

"I think," he burst out, "that the man who came last night protects them from the Law in return for work they have done for him. I thought lords were under the King to see that the Law was kept and robbers punished."

The white head was shaking slowly.

"I have forgotten," said the deep voice in a heart-broken murmur.

"It doesn't matter," said Trad at once. "But we mustn't wait, we must get away before Grandfather can come back. We've got food and money and can get a long way before anyone need see us."

"We," repeated the man. The dull vagueness which came over him as he moaned about forgetting had vanished. "Are you burdening yourself with me, child?"

Trad looked at him anxiously. Did he not want to come?

"Jokey and I would look after you until—until you can remember. And it isn't safe to stay here, truly." Unexpectedly the man laughed, a very deep pleasant sound.

"Then let us go together. But first—water. There is little on this moorland."

He had put the old leather bottle inside the rags of his jerkin and he looked around silently for the spring.

"There is some wine for you, sir," Trad told him eagerly.

The man looked at him sharply.

"Why do you call me 'sir'?"

"I think you are a knight," said Trad simply.

The man's eyes clouded but he shook his head quickly.

"No matter—no matter," he muttered. "But wine—good. Give it to me, I beg you, then come with me to the spring."

Trad was puzzled and doubtful, thinking that it would be much quicker to go to the spring by himself while the man drank the wine, but at the little sparkling pool he was told quietly to take off his shirt and kneel down. The cold water splashed over his back made him gasp and shiver.

"This will hurt more," said the deep voice, "but wine cleanses wounds and heals them. Will you bear it, child?"

Without a word Trad turned towards the man, burying his face against him as firm gentle hands sponged the open weals. The wine stung and burned like fire but Trad kept his mouth closed, and the few tears which forced themselves from his eyes were soaked up by the ragged jerkin.

"Brave, brave," came a soft murmur in his ear, and he felt almost as if he had been knighted. As he got rather unsteadily to his feet and pulled on his shirt he turned worshipfully to the first person to look after him since he could remember, and opened his mouth to ask what they should do now. It was a shock to see the alert intelligence and decision fading from the bearded face into a tired dullness.

"What now—what now?" muttered the man, staring vaguely towards the north.

"No, no, not that way," said Trad urgently, understanding that he must still at most times, as at the beginning, look after and decide for this poor old man with his wandering mind. "Come with me."

It was a wish to get help for the man which had made up his mind for him. Instead of going due south, into the wild hilly country where Grandfather might search for them in vain if indeed he thought of going in that direction at all, they would go west first. Here lay the Great Forest which most men feared, since it was dangerous in itself as well as from the desperate men who laired there, but in it lived the Wise Woman. Grandfather amused himself on winter evenings by scaring the boy with stories of the fate which would befall him if he left his grandfather's protection, and of all the stories those concerned with the Wise Woman were the most horrible. But Grandfather did not know that anyone he obviously disliked seemed to Trad a possible friend, nor did he know that the boy had already proved the falsehood of those particular stories.

It had happened when Grandfather was away once, leaving one of Diamond's band in charge of the hut. This was the only one of the robbers Trad did not entirely dislike and fear, not because the man Tawny—no gentleman but a member of the band as a superb bowman—was any less rough with him than the others, but because the brutal man had one soft spot, the large black cat Grandfather allowed to live there to complete the picture of himself as a wizard. On the sly Tawny used to feed this animal, which otherwise only got what it could catch or scavenge for itself since it would not eat bread or cheese when Trad offered it. When the robber thought no one was looking he would stroke the rough black fur or pick the cat up in his arms.

Unfortunately, Diamond had once seen him do this, and just before Grandfather and he left on this occasion he had amused himself by kicking the animal as hard as he could through the doorway, looking jeeringly at

Tawny as he did so. The robber had kept his mouth shut and pretended to take no notice, but as soon as the others had disappeared Trad had found the great rough fellow, tears running down his face, kneeling beside the limp black body of the cat.

"Is he dead?" whispered Trad, who usually knew better than to speak when he had not been spoken to.

Tawny shook his head, smearing his hands violently over his face.

"Good as, though," he said despairingly. "Three ribs broken and a hind leg. How's he going to get any food when I'm not here?"

Trad could not answer him. He wondered whether he himself could catch mice or snare birds, but if Grandfather was about he would never have the time or opportunity.

Tawny stood up suddenly.

"See here, brat. It's as much as my life's worth to leave this place—you'll have to take the cat to the Wise Woman."

Trad went quite white, more with excitement than fear, and Tawny began to coax, awkwardly.

"Forget your grandfather's tales—witch she may be, but every living thing is safe with her, nor she'll never turn anything in need from her door. She'll look after old Blackie and give him a good life—you'd like that, wouldn't you? And I'll give you—" the man paused "—nah, what use'd money be to you? I'll give you a right good meal when you get back."

Trad would have gone without that, but he could

not help saying, "What if Grandfather gets back first?"

Tawny frowned.

"Yer, that wouldn't do." He turned things over slowly in his mind.

Trad had already thought of a very good excuse, but he dared not suggest anything which showed that he was cleverer than they thought him. At last, though, when Tawny had apparently come to a defeated stop, he whispered timidly, "Master Diamond once sent me to look for a lost dagger——"

Tawny was so relieved that it did not strike him as odd that the half-wit should come up with a sensible suggestion.

"That's it! I lost—I have it! My best arrow at loose practice. And told you not to come back until you'd found it."

He selected an arrow from his quiver and stuck it through the bit of rope Trad used as a belt, then with extraordinary tenderness wrapped the black cat, struggling feebly now, in an old sack and put it into Trad's arms, at the same time giving him careful directions for finding his way across the moorland and through the outskirts of the Forest to the Wise Woman's hut.

"Dunno as you'll ever remember," he said doubtfully at the end, then shrugged his shoulders. "Won't be no loss anyway nor the cat won't be any more dead," he said brutally, but kept Trad there while he repeated the directions and pushed a large slab of cold meat into his hand.

Although it was six or seven miles of rough going to

the Wise Woman's place and the cat got heavier and heavier and crosser and crosser, Trad had not for a long time enjoyed anything as much as that solitary walk. The fact that he was defying both Grandfather and Diamond, that he was doing something useful for his friend the cat, and that he might just possibly find another friend if the Wise Woman was as Tawny and not as Grandfather described her, gave him a happiness he had not known for five years.

Nor had anything gone wrong or turned out worse than hoped. From the time he had stumbled, weary but triumphant, into the clearing where an old woman sat spinning by the door of her little wooden hut, and he had silently unwrapped the sack to show the injured animal, everything shone in his memory. The way the cat had lain, quiet and trustful, while its hurts were bound, the friendliness of the old woman without questions which he would have feared to answer, the milk sweetened with honey and the little cakes she had given him, her slow quiet agreement when he had whispered, "May he stay here?" and most of all her simple matter-of-fact, "Will 'ee stay too?" were thoughts with which he had comforted himself since at his blackest moments.

He had had to refuse, of course.

Tawny knew where he was, and he did not for one moment expect Tawny to keep the knowledge to himself if Grandfather or Diamond was really angry. Nor would he blame the man, even if he protected himself by pretending the whole thing was Trad's idea. Grandfather or Diamond would come after him and the Wise

Woman would be beaten up or even killed, and the animals which crowded her little hut would be kicked to death or left to burn when they set the hut on fire. So he had shaken his head dumbly and kissed her hand and gone running out before she could see how much he longed to stay.

Because he was turning his back on that, the journey home had been less happy, and the end of it after night fell had been difficult and exhausting. But there was one thing—life in the stone hut with Grandfather was so terrifying and horrible that nothing outside it would ever seem as bad. Even stumbling in the dark over the moorland was better than being with Grandfather, and when the moon rose and he could find his way there was something enjoyable about the strange light and the wild solitude. He was sorry when he saw the dim yellow light through the doorway of the hut, and for a little while he considered spending the night on the moor.

The thought of the explanations he would have to make to Grandfather had driven him in, and even that had turned out well, for Grandfather and Diamond had not returned and Tawny had been roughly kind. Relieved that the boy had got back through the dark, he had fed him well and sent him into his corner to sleep while he himself did some of the tasks Trad had been set. Grandfather had beaten Trad, of course, when they got back late the next day, but not as badly as he would have done if he had been able to find anything left undone. Diamond was told sullenly by Tawny that the cat was buried, and nothing had to be said about

Trad's time away. Since then, too, Tawny had treated him almost as if he were Old Blackie, slipping him odd bits of food and only pretending to cuff and kick him. On one visit he had wakened him very early in the morning and taken him out on to the moor, where he had given him his little rough bow and shown him how to tip his arrows with flint and how to practice drawing and aiming. Trad was afraid, from the thoughtful way the man looked at him sometimes, that he had guessed the boy was not a half-wit, but he almost trusted him not to tell Grandfather unless he had to, and there was nothing to be done about it anyway.

If Trad was missing, though, Tawny would certainly tell, and not only that but about the Wise Woman, so Trad had never thought again of going to her, and he would not have done so now if it had not been for the stranger. Tawny had said that she never turned away anything in need, and if she healed Blackie's broken bones she might be able to help the old man's broken wits and turn him back into the alert forceful knight who showed in flashes.

"Come with me," he said again, holding out his hand, and with a strange trustfulness the white-haired man took it.

Chapter Three

IT was a difficult journey.

Though the man had insisted on carrying the sack of food, saying with a flash of laughter that he was bigger than Trad, there were times when he hardly seemed able to carry himself. Trad, burdened with the bow and the lute and Jokey, who was only able to limp short distances on his three legs, could do little to help him. The journey which had taken Trad only four or five hours took them nearly all day because they had to stop so often to rest, and even when walking they went so slowly. It was nearly dark as they made their way through the Forest and Trad was terrified of losing the path, overgrown and rambling as it was. It was, he thought later, only the good fortune which had been his ever since the white-haired stranger had come into his life which brought them safely to the clearing and the Wise Woman's hut.

The door was shut and a faint glimmer of light showed through the rough horn window. Trad's heart sank. He could not imagine anyone in the Forest daring to open the door to a knock in the night, but he thought if the old man had to spend the night in the open he might die, so exhausted was he.

"Wait here," he whispered, and the man sank straight down with the breath of a groan.

Trad left Jokey with him as some sort of guard and ran quickly across the clearing. If he thought too long he would not dare to do anything, and as soon as he reached the door he raised his hand and knocked.

He could hear an answering movement inside and wondered who to say he was when challenged. He had just decided to say, "The boy who brought you a black cat," when the door opened and the old woman, holding a rush light above her head, stood there peering out. She looked high, as if she thought to see a man, but at once her look came down to his level, and before he could say his prepared words she exclaimed in her slow gentle speech, "Why, 'tis my little friend!" and dousing the light, gathered him into her arms, drawing him into the hut.

For a moment Trad could say nothing. The last woman to hold him in her arms must have been his mother, and it seemed in that moment that he was a little boy of four again, held in the loving arms of his bright dream world. Then he realized the truth and it was almost as bright. Here was someone who called him friend and welcomed him with love.

"Wise Woman," he whispered, not knowing what else to call her, "I have friends with me." For the first time in his memory he used the word as she had done, with confidence and love. "One is old and sick and one has only three legs."

He felt her shake with kind laughter.

"All your friends do seem to want my care." She had put down the rush light and now she carefully lit an old horn lantern. "Take me to 'un, dearling, and us shall see to their needs."

His heart bursting with joy and hope, he led her across the clearing. Jokey was alert on his three legs, guarding his master's friend, and the Wise Woman gave him a quick look before going on her knees beside the long silent figure of the man.

"Eh, eh," he heard her murmuring anxiously, "this is a big 'un. How shall us move him?"

"He can do anything that has to be done," said Trad proudly, and could not have said how he knew this. He too knelt by the man. "Sir! Sir! You must walk a few steps more."

The man stirred and the dim light glinted on his eyes as they opened. He gave a sigh which was more of a groan and then began to struggle up. Boy and old woman supported him, but it was his own will which took him unfaltering across the ten yards to the hut and into the room, where he collapsed once more, face down on the floor. Thin though he was, it took all their strength to turn him over on his back, and they could do no more than that. The Wise Woman put a pillow of softest down beneath his head and trickled what she said was strong cordial between his lips, but he opened his eyes only to shut them again and turn his head from the feeble light of the little oil lamp.

"Let 'un sleep," said the woman. "Us can't do more for him than sleep can, that medicine of all, rich and poor. Nor I can't do naught for little Three-legs, who is as well as he will ever be when he has a full belly. So what may I do for 'ee, my dearling?"

Trad sat down beside her—old Blackie leaping instantly into his lap—and with his head resting against her knee and the warmth of the cat under his hand, began to tell her all about himself.

Almost at once she interrupted him.

"Nay, nay, I know who you be, child. That wicked old granfer of yourn may think he'm hidden himself from all, but us do know more'n he do dream. Us'll never let 'un have 'ee, my dearling, never fear."

Trad did not know whom she meant by "us," but he believed and trusted her at once and entirely.

"But he may guess where I have gone," he said, anxious for her rather than for himself. "One of the—the robbers knows where I brought the cat."

"Never fret," she returned comfortably. "Us'll move tomorrow to my winter home and there lie snug as badger in holt. 'Tis not far, but if the long 'un can't walk it, I'll fetch men to carry 'un. There be many I have helped will help me."

Trad turned to look at "the long 'un." He did not quite like this way of talking of him, though that ragged hairy skinniness made what he was going to say seem absurd.

"I think he's a knight," he said bravely.

The Wise Woman gave the sleeping man a long thoughtful look.

"Very like," she said surprisingly. "There be a-many in the greenwood, sirs and lords driven out by the Lords Regent and their wicked ways."

Trad stared at her, his eyes wide with astonishment.

"The *Lords* Regent! Is there more than one of them?"

She nodded briskly.

"Ten on 'em, and never more than one good 'un, and he gone these long years, more's the pity. You found 'un on the moorland, I daresay, and saved 'un from your granfer."

Trad did not wonder how she knew this.

"Yes," he said. "That's one reason why I had to run away *now*. Wise Woman—" he spoke a little shyly "—what do you know of my grandfather?"

"More'n you do, I don't doubt," she agreed in her slow quiet way. "They do say he were Councilor to the old King till the High Prince Conrad turned 'un out for his wickedness. So in the end he came here to counsel his wicked band, bringing his only child, a sweet and pretty girl on whom 'tis said he doted."

"He *loved* my mother?" said Trad unbelievingly, remembering the way his grandfather spoke of her, always with a curse and a sneer.

"Ah, you'm too young to know the hate that love flouted can turn to. When she grew up he designed for her to marry that Diamond and she wouldna, she fled from him with your father."

"He couldn't have loved her," said Trad flatly. "Not if he wanted her to marry *Diamond*."

The wise old eyes looked at him.

"Nay, you'll never think like that 'un—'twas the best

he could do for her then, see you. That Diamond's a lord and rich—what would your granfer see against him?"

Trad was silent for a moment. Then he said hesitantly, "My mother said *my father* was a lord."

"Nor I don't doubt it," said the Wise Woman without hesitation or surprise. "That foot and that hand never come from beggar stock."

Trad looked in a startled way at his filthy hands with their broken nails and at his even dirtier feet with the thickened leather-tough soles. He could see that they were long and narrow, but that meant nothing to him.

"Nor you need never heed one word your granfer says on your father," added the old woman shrewdly, "for he never clapped eyes on 'un till he lay dead with the sweet pretty dear, and no one to guard you or save you. Ah, us have sorrowed for 'ee and would have tooken 'ee from 'un, but he have guarded you like gold."

Trad thought this over. There were many things that still puzzled him, but he was too tired to get them straight now. In a very little while he was fast asleep with his head still against the old woman's knee, and he never felt her pick him up and put him tenderly into her own bed.

In the morning he half-woke and burrowed back into the feather mattress in search of more sleep, but Jokey jumped up at him, grinning even wider than usual and licking his face until he had wakened right up. Then he tumbled out quickly, going at once to the side of the white-haired man, who was still stretched out on the floor. But he was breathing regularly and his face was quiet and peaceful, so that Trad felt much happier about him and turned at once to see what he could do to help the Wise Woman. She was not in the hut, so he made up the fire, swept the hearth, and found some bowls in which he could give water to the various animals which were in baskets or boxes around the room. He was just scrubbing the white stone at the door when the old woman came hurrying back.

"Nay, I never meant for 'ee to do this!" she exclaimed. "There's naught now but to eat your fill and then see to getting your friends to my winter home. Wake your knight then, and feed 'un."

To Trad's disappointment the tall man was worse this morning in spite of his long sleep. When he was wakened his eyes were dull and vague, and though he did obediently all he was told, even walking unaided out of the hut, he seemed dazed.

"Never fret, dearling," whispered the Wise Woman. "How can the wits mend when the body be so weak? Us'll get 'un's body strong and then see to that poor mind. Take his hand and lead 'un."

So with Jokey under his arm and old Blackie trotting behind him, Trad led his friend by twisting little paths and through thick bushes till the Wise Woman stopped in front of an enormous clump of hollies which entirely blocked their way. Without a word she dropped on her knees, crawled through tall grass and suddenly disappeared. Blackie slipped through after her and Jokey wriggled until Trad put him down, then followed the cat.

Afraid of losing sight of his guides, Trad quickly told the man to follow him and himself crawled through the grass. He found that behind it was a long low tunnel cut through the thickness of the holly, quite invisible from outside and leading to the high rock which the hollies concealed. The rock itself had been hollowed out into a wide cave with wooden doors, furnished much as the Wise Woman's hut had been, with the same collection of baskets and boxes.

Here she was evidently quite at home. On her earlier visit she had prepared a bed alongside the back wall of the cave, and here she told the man to lie down. He obeyed, and went to sleep at once. Indeed, he did nothing but sleep, and eat obediently when wakened for a meal, and sleep again for the next three days, much to the old woman's satisfaction.

"Ah, he be mending himself," she commented, and devoted herself to Trad.

He was as happy as he could imagine himself. The Wise Woman knew everything about the wild life of the Forest and he learned eagerly from her. She had not allowed him to go back to the hut in case he had been followed from Grandfather's, but the animals and other valuables were brought by various quiet men who whistled softly outside the holly tunnel before they crawled in, and who nearly all, to Trad's astonishment, seemed to know him. He only understood this when on the third day two men came together, marked by hard travel, and went on their knees to him to kiss his hand with love and gratitude. Then he recognized them as two of the travelers he had succeeded in warning away from Grandfather's hut.

He turned shyly from them to the Wise Woman, who was nodding and smiling at him.

"I told 'ee us knew on you, child. No half-wit, as 'twas said, but bold to save and clever to hide. Stay you with us and you shall be our dearling and our pride."

Trad drew a long breath.

He was learning to understand the society which the Wise Woman called "us." The desperate men so feared from outside had here formed a close-knit union in which all were equal and all helped each other. No man went shorter of food than others, or lay ill untended, or wanted for help that another could give him. No one asked who was lord or knight or peasant or thief, here they were just men, bound together against the outside world and the hardships and dangers of the Forest. In fact these hardships and dangers were so great that they had broken many who came to them from court or castle, but from the hard starved slavery of Grandfather's hut Trad looked at them without fear. He knew he would rather drown in one of the black bogs or get lost forever in the gloomy pathless depths than live in the "safety" he had been kept in up to now, while wolves and bears and wild boars, days without food and nights of bitter cold, seemed to him less cruel than his grandfather. When he was offered, as well as this freedom from the real horror of his life, companionship and love and approval, there seemed no reason at all to say no.

Forgotten on the long bed against the far wall, the white-haired man stirred and groaned.

At once Trad was at his side. The man had said nothing for three days but he had seemed uneasy if the boy was not about when he woke, and if he slept again without seeing him he lay restless and moaning.

"I'm here, sir," said Trad softly, and held water to his lips.

"He can stay too," said the Wise Woman unexpectedly.

There was trouble in her eyes and even in her slow voice, and Trad, who had never thought of the man not being allowed to stay, looked at her in surprise and distress. But before he could say anything the man had struggled up to a sitting position. He looked around, and at last his eyes were clear and seeing.

"Where—where is this?" asked the deep voice, hesitantly but not as if bewildered.

The Wise Woman had moved forward to put cushions behind him. Trad heard one of the two travel-worn men catch his breath.

"Is it—?" he turned to his companion, who leaned forward to peer into the dimness at the back of the cave.

"No—no, surely not," he muttered, though doubtfully. "This man is too old even for the father."

At the sound of the voices the man had swung around, his right hand reaching across to the place on his left hip where a sword would hang. The two men drew in their breaths sharply, and the next moment they had slipped away.

With an unusual sharpness the old woman said, "Nay, sir, you be in safety here. Tell us, then, who you be and what you want, where you come from and where you go."

The white head turned towards her and Trad saw the blank look spread over the face again.

"I—have forgotten," groaned the man, his hand going up to his head. "I think—I think I was on a quest."

The words sent a thrill through Trad but the Wise Woman snorted.

"An old man like 'ee on a quest?"

The man stared at her and his hand wandered uncertainly to the tangle of hair on his face. Bewilderment and trouble showed in his eyes.

"But I think—I think that I am a young man," he said faintly.

Trad could hardly bear it, so clear did it seem that the old man's wits were quite gone. To his surprise the Wise Woman's expression altered. She leaned forward quickly and took the man's hand in hers, looking at it closely.

"Eh, eh," she murmured. "And that may be—'tis not an old man's hand."

Trad crept closer and could see at once what she meant. This hand, though thin and transparent, had nothing like Grandfather's wrinkled blotched skin and standing-out veins.

"Is he under a spell?" he ventured.

"Nay, child, you should know from your granfer and him pretending to be a wizard, that there be no such thing as magic. He may have been ill, I don't doubt."

The old woman sounded as if she were thinking of something else. Gently now and with some respect she began asking the man the same questions all over again. The desperate effort he was making to remember was quite obvious, but at last he shook his head, letting his face fall into his hands. As he bent forward the Wise Woman laid a hand on the back of his head and began to part the thick matted hair very gently. She drew in her breath in a sharp hiss.

"Nay, how could'un live with such a wound?" she whispered.

Trad gasped too as he remembered hearing almost exactly those words before. Gazing in horror himself at the deep reddened cleft in the back of the skull which the parted hair revealed, he tugged at the woman's sleeve.

"The Lord Regent—he had Diamond attack a man, and Diamond said no man could have lived with such a wound in the head."

"The Lord Regent!"

For the second time the name had brought up the man's head alertly, but an expression of agony crossed his face and he dropped his head again, whispering, "I have forgotten."

"Nay, who can wonder?" muttered the Wise Woman.

She paused a moment in thought, then with a determined look she went to the shelf and came back with a little wooden flask. She paused again and Trad heard her say very low and sorrowfully, "I feared 'un, I feared 'un. Us'll never keep the child—but so it must be meant."

Then she touched the man on the shoulder.

"Hear me, sir." The rough country accent was hardly noticeable now. "I am the Wise Woman of the Great Forest of Taschia. If you will leave me to put you to sleep, I will ask such questions as your sleeping mind may answer which is hid from you when your mind wakes."

The man slowly uncovered his face and drew himself up. His eyes, blazingly blue, looked searchingly into hers.

"Aye," said the deep voice. "I have heard of such things. And I believe you mean no harm to me or the child. Give me your potion."

He drank it and lay back again on the bed as she had told him. In a very few minutes he was breathing evenly and deeply. Kneeling beside him the Wise Woman began again on the questions. He turned his head as if he would answer, and though his eyes stayed shut his lips moved, but no sound came from them. Patiently she asked the questions again and again, until, as the drugged sleep became lighter and more restless, she shook her head quickly, saying to herself, "Nay, 'twill not be that way." She put her hands on each side of the bearded face and held it gently but firmly till the man lay still and calm. Then she said in a voice like a bell, "Say then what you do know."

"The Tower. The Tower." The answer came almost like an echo. "The Tower reaching the sky. Climbing up and up and up. An old old man and a quest—a quest for the laughing lord."

Again Trad gasped. Grandfather had said to the

Lord Regent, "He will never be found by your laughing lord." Somehow this man was deeply concerned with the Lord Regent and whatever business had brought him to Grandfather's hut.

No more words seemed to be coming from the sleeping man, and Trad said in a whisper, "The Lord Regent paid two hundred gold coins to have this man killed so that the laughing lord should not find him."

The Wise Woman shook her head.

"These be terrible secrets, I would have kept 'ee clear if I could, child," she murmured in great trouble.

They were both startled when the man suddenly sat up. His eyes were wide open now, and yet he was obviously still asleep.

"Silver hidden in the gold—
Young man hidden in the old—
Laughing lord with weeping eyes
Bring—"

The ringing voice abruptly faltered on the last word and was silent.

"Bring what?" asked the Wise Woman urgently.

The blank blue eyes were turned on her.

"I have forgotten," said the familiar dull groan, and Trad could have wept.

The man was awake now, but confused and hazy. The Wise Woman gave him a drink of her cordial and when he had recovered they told him what he had said. He listened carefully and seemed to take it all in, but at the end he sighed deeply.

"I understand none of it," he said heavily.

"But we know more," said Trad eagerly.

The Wise Woman moved as if to stop him and then changed her mind, nodding at him to go on. He was thinking, though. It was difficult to remember clearly the words that he had not understood when they were spoken. He started slowly at the beginning.

"The Lord Regent—one of the Lords Regent—came to Grandfather's hut with the leader of the robber band. He came to pay them for killing a man three months ago, but he questioned whether the man was really dead. Diamond said that no one could have lived with such a wound in his head, though—" Trad's face lit up with pride and delight "—that man had been a champion of champions, it took fifteen men and Bron creeping up behind him with his great axe."

The man was staring at him with wide eyes. Slowly his hand went up to the back of his head.

"Aye," said the Wise Woman gently. "Such a wound as I saw never on living head. Three months agone—ah, someone have cared for 'ee since and cut the hair from the head because of the wound and the fever, and it grew again white, as I have seen afore. Do 'ee remember now?"

He shook his head.

"I remember nothing before meeting this child on the moor. I was near to death then, I think. All before is blackness, though—" he hesitated "—as by lightning flashes I see that something is there, something great and terrible. *Something I must do.*" The last words were said with startling force and he sprang to his feet.

He had sounded so sensible that it was a shock all over again to see the light fade from his face and hear the old bewildered complaint, "I have forgotten."

"Nay, sir, but 'ee must stay quiet." The old woman spoke firmly. "'Tis only in quietness the thoughts will come. Hark 'ee—this Tower you spoke on. They do say the old King be kept in the topmost tower of the City, high on the mountain where none may come to him but the Lords Regent. And the King be an old old man—nigh on a hundred if he do live still, though some say he be dead and the Lords Regent do hide it lest the High Prince Conrad come back to claim his own and punish them for their deeds."

She watched the man's face eagerly as she spoke, but there was no sign of recognition there of anything she said, and she shook her head doubtfully.

"That isn't all," said Trad quickly. "Sir, you spoke—twice—of a laughing lord. You said 'a quest for the laughing lord,' and in the verse, 'Laughing lord with weeping eyes.'" He could see that the man was still blank, so he did not ask a question but went on carefully, "My grandfather spoke of the laughing lord too. I'm not sure what he meant, but they were speaking too of the man Diamond said he had killed, and my grandfather said the Lord Regent need not fear now that the laughing lord would find him."

Still there was no response, and he cried out, "Oh sir, you are 'the young man hidden in the old,' you know of the quest for the laughing lord, and Diamond gave the Lord Regent, to prove you were dead, a gold ring with a thread of silver which he had found round your neck. There is 'the silver hidden in the gold.'"

If the man had shown any reaction at all, even a momentary brightening of the eye, when Trad spoke of the ring, he would have gone on to tell about finding the ring and hiding it, but in the man's present state he felt the ring was safer not talked about.

"'Silver hidden in the gold,'" muttered the man. "How did the rest of it go?"

> *"Young man hidden in the old—*
> *Laughing lord with weeping eyes*
> *Bring—"*

quoted Trad at once. He was sure that these were words he would never forget.

"Aye. *Bring*. There, there lies my quest—and I know neither what to bring nor where to go," said the deep voice in despair.

"Why—" began Trad eagerly, but the Wise Woman interrupted him.

"You know this, sir." Trad would never have believed that gentle voice could sound so stern. "'Tis something great and terrible—you have spoke the words yourself. Will you then take the child into it, taking him from misery to misery, from fear to fear, from danger to danger?"

Slowly the man looked from her to Trad. As if without thinking he stretched out a hand to touch the boy's back.

"That's healed!" said Trad fiercely.

"To take him—into worse?"

The man seemed to be questioning himself, doubtful and unhappy, and Trad could not bear it. He turned reproachfully to the Wise Woman.

"But I *found* him. And *my grandfather* helped to have him attacked and left for dead. Besides—" his deepest feelings broke through in a cry of excited happiness "—we should be going on a quest!"

"Nay, a quest for naught," said the old woman bitterly. Trad was surprised. It all seemed quite straightforward to him.

"A quest first to find what it is that he has to do, and then to do it," he said with great simplicity. "And I must go with him because he has no one else to look after him."

He looked up shyly at the tall man, and his heart leaped at the answering look he got.

The Wise Woman threw her hands up.

"I see that you will go, say I what I will," she sighed. "So it be meant, I doubt not." She sat down. "Well then, us must see what can be done to help 'ee."

Chapter Four

IN spite of the Wise Woman's promise of help they could not leave for three days because a terrible storm broke and kept them close in the cave day and night.

The time was used to get the man as much stronger as possible, and to make such plans as they could. They were going north after all because when Trad and the Wise Woman were discussing it in low voices while the man slept, they were startled to hear his voice, clear and confident, "To the City, of course." When he woke he could not explain his words but they dared not ignore them, and they now had to reckon on the dangers of the road north, where not only might Grandfather and Diamond be searching for Trad, but the man might be recognized either by the Lord Regent or by Diamond's band.

The answer to that came strangely, at a time they were not thinking about it. Sitting by the fire one evening Trad had idly picked up his lute and begun to pluck the strings. He could not play it, and he had only managed to restring it by watching closely a minstrel the robber band had brought with them after one particularly successful raid, but he liked the sound of the clear soft notes. To his surprise Jokey, lying asleep at his feet, woke up with a start, hopping up on his three legs and then stood up on his hind legs, pawing Trad's knee impatiently. At the same time the white-haired man, who had been sharpening a wicked-looking knife the Wise Woman had given him—though his face showed that he was engaged as usual in the agonizing struggle to remember—reached over and took the lute from him.

"By your leave, child," he said absently, and began to tune the strings, shaking his head over the state the fine instrument had got into. When he had it to his satisfaction he began to play a succession of chords and then a strong accompaniment to a wild stirring song of chivalry.

Trad listened enthralled to the deep beautiful voice but part of his attention was gradually distracted by Jokey. The little dog, still balancing on his hind legs, was turning in slow circles in time to the music. The boy seized the Wise Woman's hand and pointed in silent delight. She nodded, and when the song was finished, said, "Ah, he have been a juggler's dog, I don't doubt—thrown out, I dare say, when he lost his leg."

Trad was alight with an idea.

"We can travel as minstrels—playing the lute and Jokey dancing."

The woman looked doubtful.

"That be courtly music. 'Twould serve did you go from castle to castle, but you dursn't be seen in castle, you must travel as common folk. Common folk like other lays."

Unexpectedly the man turned towards her and laughed, his whole face altering with mischievous amusement. Then he began to play again, this time a brisk lively tune to go with a song about an old woman trying to get her pig to market which made Trad roll about with laughter, and Jokey break into a comic little jig. This was followed by a loving little courting song between a country boy and girl, and then without warning the music became a sigh and a lament. There were no words, but the music itself spoke so clearly of grief and loss, of pain and labor and failure, that Trad covered his face with his hands and cried with pity while the Wise Woman, her own pains and griefs showing in her face, stared at the player as if she had never seen him before. Large tears were rolling down his face as he played, and as he struck the last minor chord he whispered, "Alas, alas, the sorrow of the world."

There was a long silence when he had finished. Then Trad, who had found Jokey whimpering miserably and had comforted himself a little in comforting the dog, said in a subdued voice, "Couldn't we go as minstrels?"

The Wise Woman roused herself.

"Aye indeed, and live well. But I had thought on you slipping by barely noticed, and this be a Master of music—leave him touch the strings and all must heed, all eyes turn to 'un. Yet your living you must earn——"

"I have two silver pieces," Trad reminded her proudly.

She nodded.

"But who can say how long it must serve you? And none travel freely—lord and baron, merchant and priest, all will take in money or work before they give leave to pass. And indeed a minstrel may pass where others may not, paying only with his trade." She looked thoughtfully at the man. "I fear less for 'ee," she said bluntly. "So changed as you be 'tis likely none will know you. But the child—the child—that granfer 'ud know him, choose how us dresses 'un—" she broke off on the last word, her eyes suddenly startled. "Nay, nay, I never thought on—" she muttered, and then to Trad, "Would 'ee dress as a girl?"

Trad had never known any girls and had nothing against them. Understanding at once that the Wise Woman saw this as a way of making their journey possible, he agreed eagerly.

"Yes. Yes," said the man unexpectedly. "A girl child traveling with her grandfather, a broken-down minstrel—from far countries?"

" 'Twould be safer so," agreed the Wise Woman. "And there too I can help 'ee, sir."

She dragged a large chest out of the darkest corner of the cave and opened it. It was nearly empty but at the bottom were some clothes. She brought out first a dark green tunic and yellow hose. As she shook them out Trad could see that they looked different from anything he had seen before.

"There, sir, these should be outlandish enough for 'ee," she said briskly, but her hands touched the clothes with a strange tenderness as she handed them over to the man. " 'Tis all I have left of my husband's things, and he came from far parts nigh fifty years agone. Aye, and died but five years later," she added, in such a low voice that she might have been speaking to herself.

The thin bearded face was gentle with pity, but the man said nothing as he took the clothes, he only bowed as if to a great lady.

Laughing a little, the Wise Woman curtsied back to him.

"And if it please you, sir, to need a name as you travel, my husband's name were Huon—a foreign name and not unfit for a Master of music, since Huon be the King of the Fairies in France, they do say."

This time the man's knee bent to the ground in a deep reverence.

"Madam," he said in a low voice. "If you so honor me, no stain shall touch that name while I do bear it."

She looked at him quietly.

"Nay, you need not tell me so."

Trad, who thought not indeed, said with satisfaction, "Huon." Then his face fell. "Shall I have to call you 'Grandfather'?"

The man's quick look understood his rebellion against the hated name.

"Why, no." The flash of laughter came again. " 'Grandpère' for a little girl from foreign parts. Indeed, if it please you, 'Grandpère Huon.' "

Trad laughed with delight, and when the Wise

Woman, diving right to the bottom of the chest, took out a girl's dress in deep rich crimson, he could hardly wait to put it on. But after holding it up against him the Wise Woman said firmly that he must bathe first—the granddaughter of a wandering minstrel might not be clean, but she would not have the dirt of six years upon her.

Trad, who had observed with some surprise but growing liking the white-haired man's habit of washing himself all over each day since he had been strong enough to look after himself, submitted cheerfully. He had been scrubbing his hands and face but now the Wise Woman's strong old arms nearly took the skin off his knees, elbows, feet and neck, and when at last she rinsed him down with a fresh bucket of water, he stood laughing and glowing while she rubbed him dry.

She held him away from her.

"A beggar's brat, said that 'un," she murmured scornfully—and then her face changed.

She was staring at Trad's hair, still in a wild tangle but not now of a dull mud color. It leaped off his head like flames, glowing about the white transparent skin of his forehead.

"What is it?" asked Trad, alarmed.

She shook her head, glancing over her shoulder.

The man to whom she had given the name Huon had changed into the green and yellow clothes and was sitting by the fire, touching the lute strings gently, but obviously once more on the rack of a closed memory.

"Nay," she said quickly. "Your granfer 'ud know that hair anywhere. Us must change that."

She threw the cloth she had been using as a towel over his head, and hurried to the shelf where she kept her potions and remedies. Coming back with a little round wooden box she rubbed something into his hair, and with great patience and as gently as possible combed out the tangles.

"Ah," she said, looking at the result with satisfaction. Going once more to the chest she came up with a length of crimson ribbon which she tied around his hair. Carefully she lifted the dress and slipped it over his head, then handed him a brightly polished copper pan.

"Now, dearling, there 'ee be."

There had been nothing polished in Grandfather's hut and the spring had been too lively to hold a picture, so that apart from occasional glimpses in the reflections on pails of water as he lugged them about, Trad had never seen himself. Now he saw with astonishment a little pointed face with enormous startled brown eyes, delicate dark eyebrows and springing black curls. In the coppery red of the reflection he could not see the whiteness of the skin nor the flush of the delicate color in cheek and lip, but even to himself he seemed nice to look at instead of the hideous brat Grandfather had always called him.

"A lovely little girl," said the Wise Woman, nodding and laughing at his incredulous surprise. "Now what shall us call 'ee?"

Trad turned quickly and caught her hand.

"Were these—*your* little girl's?"

She nodded again, the grief too old and deep for tears now.

"She lived to be fourteen—but she were small, and you be tall like all—" she caught herself back and then went on hastily, "Her name were Trudy—do 'ee wish——"

"His name shall be called Joyous." The deep voice rang clear and confident. "For this shall be the child of Joy to many."

Startled, the other two turned, but the man was still staring straight ahead of him as if he had not spoken, and even as they looked, the expression of strain on his face became the old dull wandering look.

"What did he mean?" whispered Trad.

"All there—all there—but locked in 'un's memory and who can say what shall be the key?" muttered the Wise Woman. She seemed to make up her mind and turned briskly to Trad. "Joyeuse," she said, giving the word a pronunciation strange to him, so that he thought suddenly that perhaps she had come from far parts with her husband. "Aye, so an old minstrel might name his grandchild. I shall wash your rags, child, so that you can wear 'un beneath, and those two coins of yourn I'll sew into the waist of the dress. I have a copper coin or two will see you the first part of the way and then I don't doubt he can earn your bread and right to travel."

Trad looked wistfully at Huon's dull face, and the Wise Woman caught him suddenly in her arms.

"Never fret, never fear, dearling—power goes with you, power's about you, naught shall harm you."

He was surprised, remembering what she had said

to the man about taking him into "great and terrible" danger.

"And you said there wasn't any magic," he said doubtfully.

"And said true, child, but never durst I deny strange powers and knowings. Magic do pretend to use these powers for good or ill and that be false, but some do know and some be kept safe and some do act with power not theirn. I sought to keep you for I saw the danger into which you would go with that 'un—darkness and danger and maybe death, so it seemed. But then I knew not the powers that lie about you."

He opened his lips but she laid her fingers on them warningly.

"Nay, ask not, my dearling. Till knowledge can come to his command 'tis better to know naught—safer for both on 'ee. Even as 'tis I fear what he may say when his wits do wander—but the power must guard you."

She would say no more then, but Trad overheard her say nearly the same thing a day later, when the storm had begun to blow itself out.

The two men who had traveled hard from far in the Forest simply to give their thanks to Trad had risked the journey again while the great trees were still crashing in the fury of the summer gale. They had brought a small contribution of food and a single copper coin but this time their interest was not Trad, whom in fact they did not recognize in his glory of clean skin and girl's dress. They talked jerkily to the Wise Woman but they watched the man it was now becoming natural to call Huon as he worked at sewing a leather wallet for the journey, with frequent pauses for the useless battering at the door of his memory.

After a while they drew back, not noticing Trad in the corner behind them.

"No," said one in bitter disappointment.

"No," agreed the other slowly. "But remember, *that other* is a cousin—the look would be there. The quest is still alive."

"A sick man—his wits astray," muttered the more despondent. "Well, at least we can tell him——"

The Wise Woman turned on them with an urgency very unlike her usual slow quiet manner.

" 'Ee'll tell 'un naught. What, and have 'un drop word on it when his mind clouds, choose who be there?"

"But the time—the time," groaned the second man. "There cannot be long now, and if he is wandering alone—perhaps I should go with him——"

"You would not live five minutes near any of the Regent's guards," said his friend in sharp warning.

"Nay, the child goes with him. They will be safe—safer than you do know on."

The calm confidence of the old woman had its effect, though there was still some doubt in their expressions. She laughed a little with friendly mockery.

"Even you lords do know that that Family be protected."

"Not much sign of it these last years," muttered one, but the other disagreed at once.

"All came through the King's fault—no power will

protect against all the consequences of wicked folly. But the others are innocent. And since we ourselves are helpless we can do nothing but trust—as well in this power as in anything else."

Trad could make nothing of this, but when the men had gone the Wise Woman saw where he had been sitting, cuddling Jokey on one knee and old Blackie on the other, for they were jealous of each other. She sat down beside him, saying, in a low voice and with a glance at Huon, "What did 'ee learn, child?"

Trad looked at Huon too, and whispered.

"He's someone very important, isn't he? Those men are lords and they thought they knew him, but he wasn't the one they thought first."

"Ah, country lords those two, never at court but for the King's crowning and such—they know less than they think on," said the Wise Woman with a touch of scorn.

"But they know something about the great and terrible quest." Trad liked the sound of those words and said them often to himself. His voice sank even lower. "Wise Woman; it's to do with the King, isn't it? Is it the old old King who lives in the Tower, or is it the High Prince Conrad who sent Grandfather away and you said might come back to punish the Lords Regent?"

"Bless the child, he forgets no word," muttered the old woman. "Aye, it has to do with the King and you may say with the High Prince too. I'll tell 'ee no more than be common knowledge, for though more be whispered, who can say what truth it have? Nigh on thirty year agone the old King have fell into a fit of terrible rage against his only son, the High Prince Conrad, who have spoke for the poor against such as your granfer, and turned 'un out of the kingdom and forbade 'un to return. Where he went or if he lives still none can say for sure, though 'twas said he married the daughter of a great foreign Count and had a son. Not more'n ten years later the old King fell ill—and into his dotage, so the Lords Regent said when they seized power to rule for 'un, and so they have done in their wickedness this twenty year. And now he cannot live much longer—if indeed he live yet—and do the High Prince or his son not return to claim the throne, there be none to keep the Lords Regent from power forever."

Trad's eyes were wide and shining. Though the Wise Woman would not put it into words, he thought he knew very well who "Huon" was, and even what his quest must be. All that still puzzled him was the laughing lord. But when he asked the Wise Woman she shook her head decidedly.

"Nay, I never heard on till that 'un spoke the words. But think on, child—what would the Lords Regent be doing all these years?"

Trad was in no doubt.

"Searching for the High Prince and his son and trying to kill them. As they tried to kill *him*."

"And as they will try on, let 'un guess he live still." The woman spoke with solemn emphasis. "There be his danger—and in his state 'tis you must guard against it as so far you can. But for you, dearling, 'tis your granfer you must fear. Never will he let 'ee go willing, that I do know, and he be clever in his wickedness and his greed."

A shudder went over Trad. This was something he did not need telling.

"Would he know me—" he touched his dark curls and his girl's dress, "—like this?"

The Wise Woman sighed.

"I could wish 'ee less fair," she said to herself. "Us have just to hope and trust. And keep 'ee from 'un, dearling, flee 'un as 'twere the plague."

Trad agreed wholeheartedly. For a little while he was subdued by this reminder of his grandfather, but he soon recovered as they began to get things ready for their journey.

The Wise Woman had fashioned rough cloaks from the remains of Huon's old clothes and some bits and pieces of her own, and was providing enough food to keep them for three or four days without the need to approach people. When Trad asked anxiously how she would manage she laughed at him, saying that no one wise in the ways of the Forest went hungry in full summer. She also gave them careful directions about the safest way of going, speaking mostly to Trad. To Huon she said at the end with measured earnestness, "Do not 'ee try to remember, sir. The knowledge will come when 'tis the time for it, and to struggle do naught but cloud the mind."

Huon seemed struck by that.

"Aye, so it seems," he said slowly. "And what I say then may bring danger."

He looked at Trad as if danger there was the only one that mattered and the Wise Woman smiled, nodding at him for the first time with full approval.

"Ah, that at least you know—'tis yourn to guard the child."

The tall man looked down at her, his thin bearded face passionately serious.

"With my life," he said quietly.

Chapter Five

THE first part of their journey was quiet, uneventful and full of a happiness Trad had never known. Huon put aside, except sometimes at night when the child was asleep, any attempt to remember all that was locked in his mind, and devoted himself to Trad as the Wise Woman had done.

After six years of learning nothing except what he could pick up for himself, Trad soaked up teaching like a sponge. Huon seemed to know almost as much about wild life as the Wise Woman herself, and he knew so much more. He taught Trad to pick out tunes on the lute; the words and music of songs of all sorts, courtly and country, grave and gay, sorrowful and comic; what to say and how to behave to kings, lords and ladies, and all manner of ordinary people; how to buy and how to sell; how to bespeak a room at an inn when there was money and how to find shelter free when there was none—all this and a hundred other things filled Trad's days with enthralling interest.

The white-haired man spoke of foreign countries as if he had just traveled through them, of courts as if he had lived in them, of the miseries of the poor as if he had shared in them. Trad learned very quickly not to ask if this was true, because the slightest reference to the man's personal past brought the clouded vacant look into his eyes. Instead he asked questions differently, storing eagerly in his mind the information which came out so casually and unthinkingly.

One night as he obediently rubbed some of the ointment from the little round box into the roots of his hair—the Wise Woman had been urgent that he must never forget this—he said thoughtfully, "I ought to speak like a country person—like the Wise Woman, oughtn't I?"

Huon, who was laboriously cutting two thick sticks from a young oak, said over his shoulder without much attention, "The Wise Woman is no countrywoman. I have no doubt she is of good birth and came with her husband from foreign parts—driven out by some wickedness in her own land, perhaps."

A shadow came over his face, and Trad said quickly to distract him from the sorrow of the world, "And learned our language from the country people. But shouldn't I speak like that?"

Huon had twisted the second of the sticks free and brought them both back to their little camp, sitting down to trim them smooth.

"No need," he said absently. "All but the very poorest minstrels copy the speech of the great folk, and one who has been successful would teach his grandchild so no matter how low he has sunk. It would be safe also when traveling as a friar or a priest, since either one might be from good family, as a merchant of the richer sort, as a palmer or pilgrim, or a man-at-arms home from the Holy Wars."

All those were disguises this man himself had used, thought Trad instantly. He tried to think of a good way of finding out more, but Huon had risen to his great height.

"Come, child," he said with the quick flash of laughter Trad had come to love, "tuck up those skirts and learn how to hold a sword."

With a shriek of excitement Trad scrambled up. Having worn the skirts for two days before they started out he had got used to the feel of them around his legs—only thankful that they were not, like an older woman's, right down to the ground—but it was enjoyable to tuck them up into his belt and become a boy again.

After years of daydreaming about sword fights in which he defeated singlehanded Diamond and all his band, it was sobering to do nothing for what seemed like hours except hold the stick out in front of him while Huon patiently altered the grip of his fingers or the angle of his wrist. But he learned this, like everything else, very quickly, and it was not really long before he was faithfully copying strokes, first of defense and then of attack.

"A born swordsman, like your grandfather," said Huon, deeply intent on the boy. Trad opened his mouth to ask eagerly if he meant *Grandfather* and if so how he knew about him, but the man seemed quite unaware of what he had said.

"Come now, child, put it into practice," he said briskly, and went down on his knees, still even then considerably taller than Trad. "Now hit me."

His eyes laughed but Trad started doubtfully, troubled by the thought of that fearful half-healed wound on the man's head—what would happen if the head got hit again? He soon found that there was no possibility of that. His halfhearted thrusts met a defense as impenetrable as an oaken wall and he was soon trying his hardest, using every stroke he had been shown and a few two-handed whacks of his own which made Huon laugh as without shifting his position he caught each blow on his stick.

"Wrist *up*," he said sometimes, or "*Loosen* your grip —you are not using a hammer," and then at the end as Trad came to a breathless standstill, "Good! Good and very good!"

Trad could have burst with pride. This from a *champion of champions*! He hardly knew he had said the words aloud until Huon, who had been getting rather stiffly to his feet, turned sharply.

"Why do you call me that?" he asked with a startling bitterness. "I have not fought in a tourney since I was seventeen."

Trad held his breath, hoping for more, but instead the dreaded change came.

"Because—" said Huon, his eyes suddenly vague and

distraught, his hands shaking "—because—I have forgotten why—I forget! I forget!"

Trad tried in vain to comfort him, and though he finally lay down and seemed to sleep he tossed and turned all night, moaning or weeping. In the morning he was so broken that Trad suggested they should spend the day quietly resting.

At once the man was on his feet.

"No, no," he cried wildly, staring out towards the north. "We must not stay—time—time——!"

Remembering what one of the country lords had said about the shortness of time the boy dared not argue. With a heavy heart he began to gather their things together. Up to now they had been making a big circle around to avoid villages, but today they would have to pass through a small market town, and with Huon in this state, Trad himself would have to see to everything. When he had not known how ignorant he was he had been cheerfully confident about this journey, but now that he was beginning to understand how complicated ordinary life was he was afraid of all the mistakes he could make.

But he must just do the best he could, so with as cheerful a look as he could manage he hung the wallet with the small remnants of their food over Huon's shoulder, himself took the lute and the sticks they had used as swords, and whistled to Jokey, who was sitting hopefully outside a rabbit hole.

The little dog always whined and struggled if he was picked up first thing, but he could not walk far, and

Trad used to watch him for the right moment to pick him up. This morning he was also having to watch Huon, who stumbled on looking really like an old man, his face dull and weary, his broad shoulders bent as he leaned heavily on a tall stick, and so it happened that it was the man, looking always down at the ground, who first noticed Jokey in distress.

He stood still.

"Alas, alas," he murmured, and stooped to pick the tired little dog up.

Trad thought of Jokey as his responsibility and would never have asked Huon to share any of the trouble with him. But as they walked on he glanced sideways at the little dog cradled so gently in the crook of the big man's arm, covered in his cloak until only the pricked black ears showed, and it seemed to him that having something to look after had pierced through to Huon's true self and that the clouds hung less heavily on him. He did not talk, but gradually he began to look about him with a brightening eye, and as they came to the scattered huts on the outskirts of the town, he drew himself up with something like alertness, muttering that it must be market day. They had joined the main track now and for the first time were beginning to see people who, singly and in groups, hurried along the way they were going themselves.

Now that Huon was better the boy forgot his fears in his enormous interest in all that was going on. Huon shifted his stick and reached down to take his hand and Trad skipped along beside him quite unaware of the charming picture he made in his cloak of patches and rich crimson dress, his eyes large and brilliant with excitement beneath the dancing dark curls and gay ribbon. People glanced at the lovely child and paused to look a second time, while Trad met their glances with fearless gaiety, thinking that he had never expected people to be quite so smiling and friendly. Where were the misery and wickedness spoken about with such heavy sighs?

He did not have to wait long to see.

As they drew near one poor tumble-down wattle hut, loud wails of despair and angry curses suddenly broke out. The door was kicked open and a thickset man shouldered his way out carrying the limp body of a very young boy, while a desperate woman clawed ineffectively at his jerkin.

"There!" He tossed the boy roughly into the thick grass and nettles by the trackside. "When I say get out, ye'll get out!"

The woman, suddenly silent, fell on her knees beside the boy, who was moving feebly and whimpering as the nettles stung his bare skin.

Trad, rigid with distress, caught the sleeve of a man among a group of people who had stopped for a moment to look and were now beginning to hurry on.

"Sir—" he said, and then was unable to find more words than a gasped, "*Why*?"

The man took a casual look downwards and the hard indifference of his expression softened a little.

"Why, 'tis simple enough, for sure. The woman's

husband have died and there be none to do farmer's work in payment for the cottage. So farmer takes cottage and the woman must get out."

The woman looked up as if she had caught the words.

"Oh good people," she cried wildly, "us asked only for time. My son be sick and no food have passed our lips for three days. When I can leave 'un I can earn the few coins to pay carter to take us to my sister's—the boy be too sick to walk."

"*Time!*" said the farmer, and spat noisily, "time be money," and he strode away.

"Us have little enough to keep ourn," muttered the man Trad was still clutching. A closed mean look came over his face as he edged away, and looking quickly around Trad saw the same expression on all those who were hurrying by, though the woman's laments and explanations still filled the air. Only one very fat man, in clothes gayer but more ragged than anyone else's, hesitated for a little and then went slowly on.

At that moment a bundle was put quietly into the boy's arms. Startled, he looked down to see Jokey, wrapped right around in Huon's cloak. The man himself was on his knees, dividing the remains of their food into two small portions. One he started to replace in the wallet, but Trad crouched quickly beside him.

"Can they have all mine?" he whispered.

Huon looked at him for a moment, then touched the share he had been putting away.

"This is all yours."

Trad's face cleared at once.

"If you can do without, of course I can," he said, and picked up the few pieces to give to the woman.

For a while she did not seem to understand what he was offering her, and then she turned at once to give it to her son.

Huon was already there. He had soaked his share of bread in the small amount of wine there still was in Grandfather's flask and was patiently and tenderly feeding the sick child from his horn spoon. He glanced around at the mother.

"If you will trust me—I have been a Healer—" he stopped and looked down at his own hands in bewilderment "—I think?" he finished, his voice shaking in uncertainty. Trad feared that his mind was going to wander again but at that moment the little boy opened his eyes and cried out in fear at the strange bearded face above him. His look at once calm and confident, Huon turned to comforting him, soothing him against his shoulder and then gently feeling his forehead and his neck and leaning an ear against his chest.

"Grandpère," said Trad, remembering just in time what name he must use, and speaking with pride and love, "is very clever."

The woman was staring at them both as if they were angels from heaven. When Huon told her that the fever was breaking, all the child needed was warmth and food, she nodded dumbly.

"So we must get you to your sister," said Trad brightly. "Grandpère——?"

He had already brought out the two little coins the Wise Woman had given him and was looking at Huon for permission to give them. He got a bright flash of a smile and their other three coins were dropped into his hand.

"I will carry the child for you to the carter's," Huon said crisply, and stood up with the little boy in his arms.

People were still hurrying by, casting curious glances at the small group, and the fat man in bright clothes, who had turned back abruptly at the corner, was watching them openly. Trad, too occupied with what they were doing to notice this, picked up Jokey, who was whining and struggling to free himself from the cloak.

"Show us where to go," he said to the woman, and then practically, "but first is there anything of yours to fetch from the house?"

She shook her head.

"Naught," she said dully. "Us have naught. It all went. Farmer took our goat when my man died and priest took the chicks and every stick and clout have gone for a bite of food since."

Huon glanced down at Trad's shocked startled face, and as they walked in the direction the woman showed them he explained the custom by which on the death of the head of the household the landlord took the best beast and the Church the second best. His look warned the boy against saying the indignant words in his mind and he went on to tell the woman that his little granddaughter, coming from foreign parts, did not understand the ways of this country.

"A blessed country 'ee must have come from if there the custom be different," she said bitterly.

Huon sighed.

"We are always on the road. We see little of the lives of those living on the land but in truth I think they differ little. The people work and the lords take."

The woman looked around in terror.

"Nay, nay, 'ee must not say such words aloud," she whispered. "A-many will run and tell the lords and that do bring whipping and death."

"Alas, alas the land! No Law, no justice, no mercy."

The heartbroken murmur could hardly be heard, but the woman looked with awe at the tears of pity and grief which rolled down Huon's face.

"Few there be with even tears to spare for others," she muttered.

They had reached the place where she would wait for the carter to pick her up on his way back from the market. Taking her boy, now sleeping deeply and trustfully, she tried to find words of thanks, and when she could not, seized the man's hand and kissed it tearfully, then stooped and kissed Trad.

"Never shall I forget 'ee, never, never," she said brokenly. "Ah, if there were more like 'ee!"

Huon's face was as ravaged by sorrow as hers when he turned away, and Trad did not like to speak to him. But his own heart felt as if it was bursting with feelings he could not understand, and as he walked silently beside the man towards the town once more, his chest heaved with silent sobs.

"Child." Huon stopped abruptly and sat down on a large stone by the roadside, gently drawing Trad to stand between his knees. "Tell me what is wrong."

Stiff in his hands Trad burst out, "They don't help each other, they don't help each other! *Grandfather said they didn't*—and they don't."

He could not come nearer to explaining his horror. He had kept himself from sinking into despair in his life with Grandfather by believing that only Grandfather and his friends were wicked, cruel and greedy. Sure that everything Grandfather said must be untrue, he had pictured a world outside where, no matter what poverty or grief there might be, people were kind and gentle and ready to help each other. The society he had seen among the forest men had made this seem true, and it was not the fate of the woman, not even the behavior of the farmer and the priest, but the closed mean faces of the others as they hurried by which had shattered the picture he had clung to.

"Yes," said Huon, as if he understood everything. His blue eyes were dark with a knowledge and grief Trad had only begun to glimpse, but steady too with courage and determination. "Yet you helped me, child, and the Wise Woman helped us both."

Trad stared at him, and then suddenly saw it. Not *everyone* was as Grandfather said. He leaned thankfully against Huon's shoulder.

"And you helped that woman," he murmured.

The man sighed, but did not speak of the necessarily small help it had been. Instead he went on steadily, "And those others who did not help—where should they learn to do so? The King in his Palace, the lords in their castles, the priests in their churches think of nothing but themselves, help no one, teach no one. If the rich do not help from their plenty, is it wonder that the poor do not from their scarcity? Rather is it a marvel that there are some who do."

Remembering what the woman had said, Trad hastily looked around. No one was near enough to have heard, though the bright-clad man was again watching them from some distance away. But one word in particular had struck Trad.

He whispered, "If the *King* helped others, people would learn, wouldn't they? The High Prince Conrad wanted to help the poor, if *he* became King——"

"The High Prince Conrad is dead."

The deep voice spoke with an unthinking certainty, but when Trad looked up with a shy eagerness to ask about the son of the High Prince, the old dull look was back and the man was muttering, "I have forgotten—what is it? What is it?"

"Grandpère." Trad spoke clearly and firmly. The fat man had come closer and he was afraid of what Huon might say. "What are we going to do for money? Shall we—" he lowered his voice and guided Huon's hand to the stiff place in the waist of his dress where the Wise Woman had sewn the silver coins.

The man stared at him blankly for a moment, and then intelligence and decision came back to the blue eyes.

"No—no," he said, getting stiffly up. "Let us go on to the market—there is time enough to earn for tonight."

The noise, bustle and confusion of the market soon took Trad's mind away from sad thoughts and perplexities. Everything was new and exciting, the people themselves were as interesting to him as the stalls, and he followed Huon, hanging on to his cloak for fear of losing him, with his eyes wide and bright.

In the center of the market place, near the cross, Huon stopped, took the lute from Trad, and struck the strings. Trad saw at once what the Wise Woman had meant. Though a juggler was walking on his hands and twirling a great platter with his feet only a few yards away, and a man was bawling at people to come and see a rather mangy monkey jigging up and down on the end of a chain, the crowds had been paying little attention to them, being still intent on the serious business of buying and selling. At the authority of that single chord, though, nearly all heads turned towards them. The musician, leaning negligently against the cross itself, began a series of rippling chords to which the deep beautiful voice chanted:

"Good people, listen to my lay.
I've songs for you both grave and gay;
I'll make you laugh, I'll make you cry—
I'll charm the pigs from out the sty—
The baby from the gaping nurse—
And showers of coins from your purse!"

Some people laughed and a voice shouted, "See 'un do it, then."

A flash of laughter answered him and Huon began

the song about the old woman and her pig. Very quickly the crowds were standing four to five deep around them, applauding Jokey's little dance, watching with sympathetic smiles Trad's helpless laughter and at the end themselves roaring and rolling about at the fun of the old woman's troubles.

"Now, Joyeuse child," said Huon, quietly commanding, and played the tune of a short gay song he had taught Trad about the pleasures of each season in turn.

His voice trembling a little with shyness at first, Trad soon forgot himself in enjoyment of the song, and when as he curtsied breathlessly at the end he heard exclamations from all over the crowd of "Eh, the pretty little dear!" he was equally enraptured by the success of his singing and the joke of being taken for a girl.

Quite a little shower of coins rattled on the cobbles in front of them and he pounced on them, flushed, laughing and excited, chasing them under people's feet and the market stalls until he heard the slow tune in minor chords which Huon was now playing. It belonged to the one of Huon's songs he could hardly bear, because it was a sad little lament for a dead child. Stock-still, standing with his hands full of coins clasped tightly to his chest, he heard it with tears brimming from his eyes and trickling down his pale cheeks.

People listening to the song turned also to watch the child, and it was perhaps difficult to say whether more of them wept at the sound of the music or at the sight of the tragic little girl. Certainly as the last soft note died away there was in the very center of the market's hubbub a most extraordinary circle of quietness, where the only sound was the low sobs of the women and loud sniffs and nose-wipings from the men.

Suddenly a bold chord shattered the stillness.

"Well, good people, have I done it?" challenged Huon's deep laughing voice.

He was answered by a roar of acceptance, some rather shaky laughter and another rattle of coins. He bowed with courtly elegance while Trad, laughing again now, did the very deep curtsy in which the Wise Woman had practiced him, and then started to collect the coins, making a bag out of the front of his skirt and bringing the lot to Huon, who glanced casually at them and nodded.

"Enough, enough," he said, and sounded weary and rather vague.

With an anxious look at him Trad sat down to count the money. A shadow fell across him and he looked up in alarm, spreading his small hands protectively over the money, but the fat man in bright ragged clothes was not looking at him, his attention was entirely on Jokey. The little dog, wild with excitement, was alternately leaping up at the parti-colored legs and turning perfect circles on his hind legs, his one front paw waving gaily.

Trad, staring in astonishment, recognized first the man who had watched them on the road and then the juggler who had been performing on his hands. A *juggler*——

"Oh!" his hands flew to his mouth. "Jokey's *yours*."

The man turned. Though the fat face was creased with laughter lines, the eyes were cool and watchful.

"Jokey you call him, do you? I call him—*Jester.*" As he said the word he snapped his fingers and the little dog dropped down on to his three paws, braced himself, then flung himself high in the air to land in the juggler's arms.

Trad scrambled up, bunching his skirt clumsily to hold the money.

"You threw him out when he lost his paw," he said fiercely.

The fat man laughed.

"A good try, but you're wrong," he said coolly. "He was stolen from me—the good-for-nothing rascal who played the pipe for his dancing made off with him. No doubt *he* threw him out when he lost his paw."

Somehow Trad could not disbelieve him. Silently he turned his head away and hid his face against Huon. Jokey would have to go with his real master and he would not—*he would not* cry in front of this strange man.

Huon was looking down at him and as always when confronted with need he was alert and decisive.

"We will buy him from you," he said crisply. "Joyeuse——"

Swallowing hard, Trad opened his skirt to show the coins.

"*All* of that would barely pay for a dog of this worth. Will you give all of it?" asked the juggler coolly.

Trad opened his mouth eagerly but Huon's hand came down on his shoulder. The man was frowning.

"The child has not eaten since morning."

"So I can believe." There was an odd dryness in the tone. "Two coins, then, for bread for the child, and the rest for the dog."

Huon nodded, and startlingly the man burst out laughing, all his rolls of fat shaking.

"Heaven guards fools and children, they say—not that I have ever seen signs of it. Suppose I take your money—you can see that the dog knows he's mine. A whistle in the night and there you are—no dog, no money. *Now* will you pay me for him?"

Bewildered, Trad gazed at him and then looked up at Huon. A little smile was half-hidden in the depths of the curly white beard and Trad's heart leaped up. He still did not understand, but if Huon thought it was all right—he turned at once to the juggler, offering his open skirt.

"Take it all," he said eagerly. "I can do without food and Jokey will be able to find *something* for himself among the stalls."

"Not so fast, not so fast. I have a different plan to offer."

That little smile was still on Huon's lips.

"So I thought," he murmured.

The fat man gave him a rather startled doubtful look and then began to speak fast, telling them that without the dog, whom he himself had trained from a puppy, his act had been less successful and he had fallen on hard times. Also he needed music, and then he would have an act without compare.

Unexpectedly Huon laughed, a deep sound of genuine amusement.

"And will the addition of a juggler improve *our* act?"

Again the juggler seemed disconcerted, and Trad thought that he must have seen Huon in one of his vague moments and supposed he would be easy to manage. But he quickly recovered himself.

"At least it will make sure that you get something to eat," he retorted. "Already today I have seen you give away all your food, all your money, and ready a *second* time to give away all your money. Heaven knows how you have got as far as this."

"No doubt It does," agreed Huon dryly. "So you will join us to protect us?"

On the whole this seemed to Trad a good idea, even apart from making sure that Jokey stayed with them. But he was puzzled to know how they could tell whether the juggler was to be trusted. Again he looked up at Huon and saw that he was looking steadily at the fat man. At first the cool light eyes avoided the brilliant blue ones, then suddenly they turned to meet them.

There was a very short silence.

"Agreed," said Huon quietly.

The juggler bent to put Jokey into Trad's arms.

"Agreed," he said rather huskily.

Chapter Six

THE addition of Marlo the juggler to their party was as useful as Trad had hoped. He took them straight away to an inn where they could sleep in the straw of the loft for a quarter of the price of dirtier beds inside, and then as Huon seemed on the point of collapse he suggested leaving him there while he himself showed "the little girl" the sights of the town.

"Grandpère, may I go?" asked Trad, half doubtful, half eager.

Huon roused himself momentarily to give the juggler a keen look.

"Yes, yes," he muttered. "He can be trusted, as far as" his voice trailed away into a vague blur of sound.

Marlo looked at him oddly but did not comment. He told Trad to hold tightly to his hand, and showed himself an interesting and amusing companion. He asked few questions, but Trad thought it best to tell quite quickly the story he and the Wise Woman had prepared.

"My father and mother are dead," he said, and let the tears he had learned to shed so easily trickle from his eyes. "And Grandpère is taking me to the City where we have relations. But Grandpère has been ill and he is so old he is forgetful, and then I have to look after him, because sometimes he thinks he has forgotten something very important and says strange things, and people think he is mad but he isn't."

"Mad, no," said Marlo thoughtfully. "In a distress of forgetfulness."

The phrase struck Trad as bitterly true and he looked at the fat man with growing respect.

"And old and ill," added the man briskly. "But we'll look after him, little girl—Joyeuse, he calls you, doesn't he? A strange name from a strange man—but a Master of music, without a doubt."

Trad nodded eagerly and found the man's look on him watchfully.

"Yet," he said softly, "it is in my mind that I saw your Grandpère two years ago—but *then* he was a Healer and young."

For a moment Trad did not know what to say. He remembered Huon calling himself a Healer and then becoming confused, and it seemed likely enough that among his disguises he had passed himself off as one of the Healers who traveled through countries and from country to country, valued and welcomed by all. But it was going to be terribly dangerous if Huon could be so easily recognized by those who had known him before his wound.

"How could Grandpère have been young two years ago?" he whispered, his lips trembling.

His distress was enough like innocent bewilderment to convince the man, who shook his head and muttered to himself, "Not so like, perhaps, but those eyes—those eyes! Yet that other was young—" he looked abruptly at the child. "Might it have been your father?"

"Oh no." This was something Trad could sound certain about. He did not say that his father had been dead for six years, since that did not fit in too well with his tale, but with absolute conviction went on, "My father was a minstrel. The lute is his. Only," he added hastily, "Grandpère has it because his was stolen while he was ill."

Marlo snorted, diverted into a bitter comment on the helplessness of wanderers when they were ill.

"Only those who travel with you will protect you in a world of thieves," he concluded meaningly and Trad glanced up at him, sparkling with laughter.

"Oh yes, I think we're very lucky you will join us," he said demurely.

"Lord in heaven, what I could do with a child like this!" muttered the juggler.

Alarmed, Trad snatched his hand away, and the man laughed abruptly.

"No, I'm not going to steal you from your Grandpère. As he said, I am to be trusted as far as—what? At least with children. But your Grandpère wastes you, though you sing very nicely. Will you let me teach you to dance?"

Trad agreed eagerly, though thinking regretfully of

the somersaults and cartwheels which his skirts would prevent him learning, and when they got back to the inn Marlo gave him his first lesson. He was delighted with the child's quickness and natural grace, and considerate enough to stop at once when he saw that "she" was tired after the excitements and feelings of the day.

Yawning, Trad sat close to Huon, who lay in the straw with his eyes shut, and watched with delight as Jokey demonstrated a series of tricks the boy had never guessed at. He lay still and apparently unbreathing at the command "Dead dog!" and leaped up like quicksilver at a certain whistle; he caught in his mouth and threw with a quick jerk of the head a leather ball stuffed with feathers; he "counted" a number of coins, and barked "yes" or shook his head "no" in answer to questions.

"Clever, clever boy," murmured Trad, lying back drowsily. Huon's arm came around him and with a sigh of perfect happiness the boy curled up beside his guardian and slept without stirring until the morning.

The next few days, in fact, stayed in Trad's memory all his life as a time of perfect happiness. The weather was beautiful without being too hot; there was no shortage of food because Marlo spent their coins shrewdly and they could get more whenever Huon would stop to give a show; even the urgency which, rather to Marlo's annoyance, drove Huon on towards the City with as little pause as possible gave a bite of excitement and importance to their journey. Though any suggestion that they should linger in some particularly generous and appreciative place would throw

Huon into wild agitation for a little while, as long as they were traveling onwards he was the enchanting companion of the first few days. Nor did the presence of Marlo spoil things. Nearly as widely traveled as Huon, he had his own tales of adventure or interest, and though the miseries and wrongs which moved Huon to grief produced in the juggler an ugly savage bitterness, he could also be so funny that even Huon had to stop and sometimes sit down, helpless with laughter.

Trad came to believe that the times when Huon gave himself up wholly to those deep roars of mirth were like medicine, each one helping to strengthen and steady his mind, and as a return for them he served Marlo as eagerly as he looked after Huon.

He hardly noticed, because being cared for was something he had been taught not to expect, how both men watched and guarded him, nor with what delight they filled that fresh thirsty mind. He preferred what Huon taught him because sometimes Marlo's bitterness reminded him just a little of Grandfather, but he enjoyed very much being taught to dance and even more being shown how to put Jokey through his tricks. Also he could ask Marlo some of the questions he dared not ask Huon. A casual reference by the juggler early one morning to the King's highway gave him the chance to ask innocently, "Shall we see the King on the highway? There is a King of this country, isn't there?"

"There is a corpse in a castle and ten uncrowned Kings gobbling up the land—take your choice," said Marlo harshly.

Trad looked at him wide-eyed, and more gently the man began to explain to him what the Wise Woman had already told him about the King's great age and the seizure of power by the Lords Regent.

"But has the King no son?" asked Trad wonderingly.

The juggler glanced around hastily and lowered his voice.

"He had one, but he is probably dead. If *he* had a son—Heaven help him! The Lords Regent have long arms. I wouldn't myself give two farthings for his life." He stopped, his expression a curious mixture of doubt and hope. "*If* he lived—what a King that might be! A *king* who had lived among the people and knew something of their lives, their needs and their miseries!"

"A laughing lord with weeping eyes," whispered Trad, his own eyes brilliant as he thought of Huon, and then stopped aghast.

Marlo's fat face had gone white, almost gray, with terror and he now caught the child to him, covering his mouth with a plump hand.

"For Heaven's sake, child, do you want us all hanged? Where, in the name of all angels and devils, did you hear that?" he breathed jerkily.

Trad was suddenly desperately frightened. He did not trust the man quite enough to tell him the truth, and not to answer would simply add to his suspicions. He thought now that Marlo had for the last day or two been looking with too much interest at Huon's hands —not an old man's hands, as the Wise Woman had said. He must—he *must*—get his attention away from Huon.

"I heard it—from a peddler," he gasped, almost sobbing. "A—tall slim man with golden hair."

Not until he had said the words did he remember the Lord Regent hissing them in his ear that dark night.

Slowly Marlo let go of him.

"God in Heaven," he said almost soundlessly. "God in Heaven! Can it be——?"

Trad clutched his sleeve, looking around as he did so to make sure they were still unheard.

"Why is it so dangerous?" he whispered urgently.

Looking around himself, Marlo went down on his knees, bringing his mouth close to the child's ear.

"They say old King Tancred himself stood up at the last Council meeting—he who has neither stood nor spoken in public these twelve years—and said a verse with those words. I know only one other line—'Silver hidden in the gold'—well, all old enough to remember the High Prince Conrad know what that means. Prince Conrad or his son, they say, is on his way back to claim the throne when the old man dies—and the old man knows it. The Lords Regent are mad with fear and anger—to say anything like those words means prison or death. Where was this peddler, child—where, where?"

Trad was frightened again by this urgency and unwillingly suspicious.

"Over the border," he said quickly. "Many days' journey back."

Marlo sighed and got up slowly. Trad dared not ask him now what "all who remembered the Prince Conrad" knew about the silver hidden in the gold. All he could venture was, "Are all the Lords Regent bad?"

The juggler, the folds of his face looking depressed and sad, said absently, "There was one not so bad—they had to appoint him because he was cousin to the old King. But he died twelve years since and *his* son disappeared at the same time." He looked up suddenly. "Nay, nay," he muttered. "Strange—*there* was the laughing lord! His name was the Lord Hilarion, which means laughter, and they say he was very young and gay. What part has he in this?"

Trad was even more puzzled. As he understood it, Huon's quest was to find the laughing lord, yet it seemed more natural the other way around. Twelve years ago—and what about the ring? If the one Huon had carried was only half a ring, as Grandfather thought, where was the other half? Did the laughing lord perhaps carry it, and was that why Huon must find him?

Marlo had bent down to him again.

"Child, who is your grandpère?" he whispered.

Trad braced himself.

"I don't know," he said, his eyes steady because this was true as far as it went—he need not add what he guessed.

The juggler's face fell again.

"And who are *you*, child?" he pressed, with less hope.

"I don't know," said Trad again, and this time his lips trembled because it was entirely true.

"Maybe you don't, maybe you don't," Marlo said

grumblingly to himself. "Maybe it's all locked up in the mind of that grandpère of yours. But I know this —you are dangerous company, both of you, for a timid man like me." He saw Trad's startled gaze and laughed abruptly, without amusement. "Forget it, forget it. And get your grandpère going, or we shall be late for the fair."

They were making for a large town less than two days' journey from the City, where the Midsummer Fair was being held. Trad had supposed that a fair was only a slightly larger market, to which he was becoming accustomed, and he was overwhelmed by the size, the gaiety and the variety that he found.

Their money was low, so after paying their dues they set up their pitch at once, Huon's authoritative chord claiming its usual attention. With a crowd willing and eager to be amused they were an instant success. It had been agreed that Marlo and Jokey should always open the act, and the fat man's extraordinary agility and bounce, his skill in keeping a dozen balls, platters and knives in the air at once, and the little dog's cleverness and courage got their fair share of applause before Huon took over. Huon played for the juggler with a muted skill which left all the attention for the man, and this day Trad for the first time was in charge of Jokey. The finish, where the "little girl" and the dog danced solemnly opposite each other while Marlo turned lightning cartwheels around them and between them and over them, brought a good scattering of coins, and then just before the people turned away Huon struck up one of his apparently endless repertoire of comic songs.

Marlo had suggested that he made them up, sometimes on the spot, but Trad found this hard to fit in with his heroic idea of Huon. On the other hand, Huon usually seemed to enjoy the jokes as much as his audience did, and today he did not change the mood to sad music. Trad sang one gay little song, and Huon finished by sweeping all their hearers into a Midsummer carol known throughout the country. There was even some silver among the coins that Marlo and Trad gathered up, and with a laughing glance at them Huon said gaily, "Now a fairing for Joyeuse!"

Startled and delighted, Trad was led to the stalls where sweetmeats, toys and a richness of ribbons, jewelry and ornaments dazzled his eyes. They bought him some gilded gingerbread and both men laughed at his expression of ecstasy at the first taste; they bought him a new hair ribbon and a little leather purse; then, turning to the toy stall, Marlo said gravely, "Now all little girls want their own wooden babies."

Trad looked in dismay at the stiff little wooden puppets with their staring painted cheeks and eyes, and wondered glumly if all little girls did indeed like them. He looked out of the side of his eye at Huon, who was thoughtfully examining some daggers with ornamental handles, lovely little weapons no longer than his hand but with keen bright blades. Then he sighed and brought his reluctant attention back to the toy stall. He was just going to thank Marlo as gratefully as possible and accept a doll with what pleasure he could assume, when he caught sight of something half-hidden among the piles of dolls.

"Look, look!" he cried, seizing the juggler's hand. "There's Jokey!"

Jokey, comfortably in his usual nest in the front of Marlo's jerkin, poked his head out with a little inquiring bark as Trad burrowed among the dolls and pulled out a rather shapeless little bundle of fur only recognizable as a dog by the pricked black leather ears and bright button eyes. But it was soft and silky and Trad stroked it lovingly before asking rather hesitantly, "Might I have it instead of a wooden baby?"

Marlo, grinning broadly for some reason, agreed and began to bargain with the stall keeper. Before he had finished Huon turned and put one of the little daggers into Trad's hand.

"Even a girl child may need a sting," he said dryly to Marlo's sharp look, and the eyes of the two men met for a moment in some unspoken understanding.

Feeling almost dazed by this accumulation of treasure, Trad stood there with his hands full and his heart even fuller.

"Thank you," he whispered, blinking because he thought he was going to cry. "Thank you very much."

Marlo rescued him.

"And now," he said briskly, having beaten the stall holder down to half the price first asked for the fur animal, "for a fairing for *us*. At the Crown, Grandpère Huon, don't you think?"

Huon laughed and agreed, so they pushed their way through the crowds to the town's chief inn. Here the crowds were nearly as great and while the men waited to be served with their ale Trad slipped away into a corner to examine his new possessions.

The dagger would have to be hidden and he ran his hands adoringly over it before working it down the front of his dress, making sure that it was safely held in the waistband of the breeches he was still wearing underneath. He put the new ribbon into the little purse and hung that from his belt, then held his toy Jokey against his cheek, loving the softness and warmth of it, and dreamily going over the delights of that day.

He jumped as the hostess of the inn, who had been bustling about getting redder and redder, put a heavy hand on his shoulder. She now looked flustered to the point of distraction.

"You be the juggler's little girl, bain't you? Will 'ee help me? You see how 'tis—I be run off my feet and here be these important guests and no one to send in with their wine and I dursn't keep them waiting. A nice little girl—and *clean,*" she added with obvious surprise as she took a further look at him. "You'll be a dearie, won't 'ee?"

Trad was very ready to help, and delighted at the thought of seeing some "important people" close to. He took the tray with a bottle of wine and two silver tankards, carried it carefully along the dark passage at the back of the inn, and put it down on a settle while he knocked at the door. He thought he heard a voice saying "Enter!" and opened the door before picking up the tray and going in.

After the dark passage, the sun streaming into this

small private parlor nearly blinded him, and he paused for a moment.

Then he nearly dropped the tray.

A voice said with well-remembered softness, "And so the ring is lost."

Trad gulped and clutched the tray, fighting the temptation to run away at once. He could see now, and to his growing horror not only was Diamond lounging against the latticed window, but the Lord Regent he knew was sitting at a table beating his fingers on it in a rapid angry tattoo.

He grunted without speaking and Diamond said negligently, "And you're quite sure the old man hasn't got it?"

"No man conceals the truth after a fortnight in my dungeons," said the Lord Regent flatly, and Diamond laughed, a soft evil purr. At the same time he turned his head and saw Trad. His eyes narrowed and then he shrugged his shoulders, obviously dismissing the little girl as unimportant.

"Put it down and get out," he said sharply.

Trad sidled forward, his bare feet noiseless in the thick rushes, slid the tray on to the table by the Lord Regent, and just remembered to make a breathless bob of a curtsy before scuttling away.

But his fear had somehow turned to a fierce determination to hear what they were saying. He dared not leave the door open behind him and there was no keyhole, while the door fitted with unusual closeness. Yet he could hear a murmur of voices as he stood there and by concentrating his attention until he felt like nothing but a large ear, he traced it to a spot high up on the wall to the left of the door.

In a moment he was up on the settle and feeling the wall with light fingers. They touched a roughness and then a hollow—a knothole left in the wood which had at sometime lost its center. By leaning his ear closely against it he could hear every word.

"The half-wit might have picked it up—they are like jackdaws."

It was a casual suggestion from Diamond, and though it made the boy's blood run cold, the Lord Regent dismissed it impatiently.

"He would have given it to his grandfather—he was terrified of the old man. I believe it must have jerked from my pouch on the road. No matter, as long as it is not—" he stopped abruptly, then added in a different tone, "Are you sure that man is dead?"

"As sure as one can be," drawled Diamond.

"We thought we were sure that old dotard could not speak," said the Lord Regent bitterly. "To break a twelve-year silence—and to break it *so,* in full Council! Do what we will, that prophecy has run through the country like fire."

"Prophecy?" Diamond's tone, never noticeably respectful, held an open sneer. "We who have known a Master Wizard—" again came that evil purr of laughter "—need surely never believe in magic of any sort."

"You speak like a fool," snarled the other man. "It is not what we believe but what the people believe that matters. I tell you that if a beggar enters the Gate before sunrise during the King's Week with any trumpery ring on his finger, he will be proclaimed as King."

"Alas that you are not loved!" The mockery was quite unconcealed. "So that for a week after the King's death you must prevent the High Prince Conrad entering the City between the hours of sunset and sunrise or lose your power. Why—may I ask—do you not simply go on concealing the death of our Sovereign Lord, King Tancred the once-Glorious, until the week is over?"

"Because," growled the Lord Regent, "for the *people* the week starts when the death of the King is announced. We have delayed the announcement only until we could arrange to have the way guarded. It is *seventy-five years* since this ritual nonsense was gone through—curse the long memory of the poor! At least Conrad is dead—we have learned that at last. But he had a son whom he called Manfred——"

"Ah!" said Diamond softly. "A champion of champions—or a tall slim man with golden hair?"

"Where did you learn that?"

The voice held terrible danger but Diamond was quite unperturbed.

"My ears are remarkable, my lord, I heard what you whispered to the half-wit. So you are inclined to think that old Master Wizard is playing some game of his own? Likely enough. Is it this slim man I am to look out for? Or the ghost of the champion? You tell me too little if you want the job done properly."

"I have told you more than the other Lords agreed

to," said the Regent angrily. "Nor can I tell you more—the description is twelve years old, some of that Family broaden out as they get older.

"You are to stop *anyone* who approaches the City Gate between sunset and sunrise. The gates must stand open and the trumpeters must be there, and all the idle poor of the City *will* be there—rot them!—so no one is even to come within sight of the Gate. Do you understand?"

"I stand to lose as much as you," pointed out Diamond dryly. "No King will be as—understanding—to people like me as our beloved Lords Regent have been. I shall allow no one to approach the Gate, no man, woman, child—or ghost. Him at least I shall be sure of. No one can fight to the death as we did and fail to recognize his foe in any guise."

Trad, who had been absorbing everything with a strained attention devoted to remembering it word for word rather than understanding it, suddenly realized the meaning of that last sentence. He trembled with shock and fear. If Diamond would really recognize Huon *whatever* he looked like——

The Lord Regent had unexpectedly broken out into a shout of rage.

"May the old man rot in hell! Twelve years ago he must have planned this—somehow smuggled the half ring to that young fool with his light laughter and his lute, I always hated him, and sent him out in secret——"

"The King must have both halves, must he?" said

Diamond thoughtfully. "And I suppose the High Prince had taken one half with him."

"One of the ancient secrets of that House—we only learned of it from the old fool's babbling in a fever a few weeks ago," said the Lord Regent morosely. "I tell you—magic or no magic—that Family has power. When he spoke at the Council it was as one who *knew.* And he died smiling, saying—to whom, in God's name!—'I have kept my word.' Do not think this will be easy—*that Family has power.*"

He spoke with such a fury of conviction that even Diamond sounded a little shaken.

"Have no fear, my lord—*no one* shall approach the Gate. And if possible we shall pick up anyone dangerous before they even get near it."

There was movement as he spoke, and Trad only just understood in time that the man was coming to the door. To jump straight down from the settle would mean that Diamond would find him immediately outside the door, so without a second's hesitation he flung himself backwards in one of the somersaults he had copied from Marlo and practiced whenever he had a moment to himself. He landed sprawling on the floor at the far side of the corridor and was just picking himself up when Diamond pulled the door open.

The sunlight streaming out showed up the crimson dress, and with an oath the man leaped forward and seized the child by the shoulder.

"What are you doing here?" he said in his softest, most dangerous purr.

Trad did not yet know about himself that in moments of extreme danger his mind worked with extreme speed, and always towards extreme boldness. It seemed to him that it was without thinking that he opened wide eyes at Diamond, fluttering the eyelashes as he had watched girls doing since he had first come across them.

"Why, sir," he said in a high excited voice, "I did hear 'ee say to the other gentleman that the ring be lost. 'Twas the big red ring on 'un's finger, I says to myself, and if so be 'ee find it for 'un, my girl, they'll give 'ee a present, being generous gentlemen. So I has been looking over every inch 'ee have gone by."

Nothing could have been less like the scared half-witted urchin of Grandfather's hut, with his downcast eyes and whimpering mutter, and certainly Diamond lost at once even his smaller suspicion of listening at the door.

"I'll give you a present all right," he said with a careless smile, and put a finger under the child's chin to lift its face for a kiss.

Trad could feel himself stiffening all over—if Diamond actually kissed him he thought he would be sick. But he was saved by an angry exclamation from the Lord Regent, who had followed Diamond out.

"God's Blood, man, is this a time for playing with girls? Get on with your work."

The ugly look Diamond gave his superior as the latter shouldered past him to the back door of the inn made Trad shake, but he took the opportunity to wriggle free from the man's grip and flee towards the kitchen. He dared not lead Diamond into the drinking room where Marlo and Huon probably still waited for their ale, but in fact Diamond uttered another oath and followed the Lord Regent.

Then at last Trad could go find Huon.

Chapter Seven

HUON'S great height made him easy to see even in such a crowd as still thronged the inn, but reaching him was a different matter.

Trad started politely, saying, "By your leave, sir," as he tried to edge past men already at the roaring stage of drink, but no one seemed to hear him and at last he was pushing, shoving and wriggling with all his strength. Every moment he was held back seemed to him to add to Huon's danger, and he got quite frantic. Crimson and sobbing, he was desperately contemplating taking out his dagger when there was a soft, "Now, now," above him and the next moment he was high up in Huon's arms, caught into that strength and comfort.

"What is it, child?" said the deep soft voice.

His arms tightened stranglingly around the man's neck.

"Huon, can we go—at once, at once?" he gasped.

Without another word the tall man turned and began to make his way to the door, still carrying the child.

The throng was as thick as ever and Huon did not seem to use any force, but he went through the crowd without pausing.

At the inn door they met Marlo, who had obviously been looking for Trad, for his face cleared when he saw him. Then as he saw too the tear-stained face and heaving chest his expression darkened and surprisingly a sharp bright knife appeared in his hand.

"Has anyone dared—" he began in a snarl very unlike his usual cool high voice.

Huon held the child away from him to look at his face.

"No, no," cried Trad, frantic once more at the thought that they might waste time trying to find someone who had hurt him. "No one touched me. But we must get away at once. I heard—I heard—" he could not think for a moment how to begin telling them all that he had heard. And some of it probably ought not to be told in front of Marlo anyway "—the King is dead," he said in a little gasp.

"Dead?" said Marlo sharply and at that moment they heard the bells begin to toll, first from the big church in the market place, then in the other little churches and chapels and at last, faintly, from the nearer country churches.

Huon's hold slackened and Trad wriggled down to the ground. He looked hopefully up at the man's face, thinking that this might be the key the Wise Woman had spoken of which would unlock his memory, but the bearded face was very grave and withdrawn, as if the thoughts brought by this death were totally private.

A strange stillness was creeping over the town, gradually swallowing up the noises of the fair as people began to realize what the widespread tolling meant. They stood quite still, looking vaguely in the direction of the sound, their faces shocked and fearful rather than grieved. The King now dead had reigned for seventy-five years, but even in the days of his strength he had been admired rather than loved, and for the last twenty years he had been no more than a name. Most people could hardly remember seeing him, and the name that was occasionally muttered—with the usual glance over the shoulder—was not Tancred but Conrad.

"Dead," said Marlo again in a low voice. "Then all the approaches to the City will be guarded. You cannot continue your journey now."

Huon turned. He did not look wild, but behind his determination was a curious emptiness.

"We *must* go to the City—though—I have forgotten why."

"Heaven help us," muttered the juggler as if he really meant it.

"And quickly, quickly," sobbed Trad. "There are men who know him."

Marlo looked at him sharply but did not ask any questions. He stood for a moment in deep thought.

"You had better come with me," he said, but there was a certain doubt and reluctance in his voice which alarmed Trad. "I can take you—at least nearer the City." His own voice seemed to have made up his mind. He shrugged his shoulders and said with brisk decision,

"It will mean food for at least three days, since we must avoid all dwellings. And water. In this dryness we cannot rely on the streams. If you will see to the food, Grandpère Huon, I will get us a water skin."

He gave Huon a keen look, seemed to be satisfied that he was able to do what had been suggested, and himself went off quickly. The money they had earned that day had at once been divided between them and Huon made for the food stalls, where he bought bread and cheese. He inquired about a certain dried sausage and was directed to a shop in the market place.

Trad, trotting along beside him, found to his surprise that he was still crying. The shock of the danger from Diamond and the Lord Regent, the delay in reaching Huon, and most of all that dismaying emptiness in Huon's reaction had been too much for him. He sniffed as quietly as he could, rubbing the tears away with his sleeve when he thought Huon was not looking, but his forlorn tear-smeared face was more like Trad's of Grandfather's hut than it had been since he had run away.

He discovered this alarmingly in the next few minutes.

Huon had gone into the dark little shop and Trad had slipped his hand out of his and stayed behind. He was trying to work out ways of protecting the man in his great danger, and was thinking regretfully of his bow left behind at the Wise Woman's cave. Even with flint-tipped arrows it was more likely to kill a man than his little dagger, and unconsciously he fell into the archer's attitude, fitting an imaginary arrow to an imaginary bow and drawing as Tawny had taught him, with a strong even pull.

"God's Body!"

The loud rough exclamation brought him shatteringly back to reality. He looked up—straight into the face of Tawny himself.

There was no doubt that the man recognized him. Amazement and certainty were both in his face, and Trad thought wildly of trying to silence him with his dagger—but it would never get through the archer's padded leather jerkin—and Tawny had been kind to him——

"Tawny!"

This was Diamond's voice, raised to an unusual bellow to reach across the crowded market place, and Trad gave himself up for lost. He had better go quietly, hoping that Huon would not be brought out of the shop to be recognized by Diamond—and perhaps Diamond wouldn't mind even if he *had* run away from Grandfather, he could pretend he was with Marlo, Marlo might be clever enough to back up this story——

His frantic thoughts were interrupted. Tawny had turned his head slightly towards his captain and when he turned back his face was quite blank. He looked at Trad as if he had never seen him before, said roughly, "Get out of my way, little girl," and pushed him hard, sending him flying into the doorway of the shop, before striding off through the crowd to the place where Diamond and two mounted men-at-arms were waiting impatiently.

Trad recovered his balance and, too thankful to try

to understand what had happened, flung himself at Huon, who had just finished buying the sausage.

"Grandpère, wait, wait," he gasped. "May I choose —may I ask—would the kind butcher have some little pieces or bones for Jokey?"

He opened his new purse and offered Huon the coin Marlo had slipped into the purse "for luck."

"A fairing for Jokey?" he said pleadingly, fluttering his eyelashes as he had done for Diamond.

Huon's look, surprised at first, grew thoughtful, but the little fat butcher was enchanted. He took a satisfactorily long time collecting little scraps of meat from different corners of the shop and at the end even refused the coin, suggesting a kiss instead. Trad quite willingly put his arms around his neck and gave him a shy little kiss, and the butcher took another few minutes telling Huon what a delightful little girl his granddaughter was.

Huon agreed, and himself talked of the child's kind heart, her devotion to the little three-legged dog and her care for himself. He was only interrupted at last, obviously to the butcher's regret, by the entry of another customer, and even then he paused well inside the doorway, murmuring so that only Trad could hear, "Danger?"

Trad ran outside and looked carefully all around the market place. There was no sign of Diamond and his followers and he came back saying quietly, "Not now."

As they made their way to the Crown—since no arrangement had been made in the hurry they expected Marlo to meet them there—Huon picked Trad up again, as if the "little girl" was tired, and Trad could whisper to him, "It was the man who fought you. He said he would always know you again."

"Very like," muttered Huon.

"And—oh Huon!" A sob interrupted Trad, but he instantly suppressed it. He would *not* cry again now. "It's him who's guarding the ways into the City. How are we going to get past him?"

Huon's hold tightened and to Trad's joy he heard the deep pleasant laugh.

"What must be done can be done," said the man firmly, and with new confidence and hope Trad scrambled down and ran to Marlo, waiting outside the inn with obvious nervousness and impatience.

"I've got *such* a treat for Jokey," he said gleefully, and even Marlo relaxed a little and led the way out of the town by alleys and byways with a fair cheerfulness.

In the next three days they traveled hardly more than a normal day's journey. They avoided all roads and even footpaths, so that they had to fight through thick undergrowth, tread cautiously over marshy land, or trudge wearily over rough moorland. They made wide circles around even isolated dwellings and lay up in any shelter they could find at the first sign of a living person.

Twice they caught glimpses of armed patrols, but both Marlo and Huon seemed expert at this deadly game, and slowly but steadily they made their way towards the City. The ground was rising all the time, but because Marlo led them as far as possible in clefts and gullies, it was not unitl the third day that they got, as they topped a little rise, their first full sight of the City on its mountain.

Trad, who had been running ahead with Jokey, came to a stunned standstill.

Marlo had described the City, but the words had meant very little to him, since as far as he knew he had never seen a mountain, and he had been picturing a larger version of what was within his experience—a town on a hill. But this mountain, on whose lower slopes they were, towered above them, and the great walled city built in three tiers on the upper half and crowned by the milk-white castle whose topmost tower blotted out the crest of the mountain and seemed indeed to touch the sky, was like nothing he could have imagined. And yet——

"I have seen this before," he said aloud, though not to either of the men.

Marlo looked at him curiously but Huon, himself staring at the Tower, did not seem to hear.

"I remember," he said in a voice as strange from him as those words, "I remember. I climbed up the outside of that Tower and he promised to stay alive until I brought—I brought*—and I have failed.*"

Quite quietly he sat down on the ground and laid his head down on his knees in a gesture of utter defeat.

Trad could not bear it. Kneeling beside him he clutched his arm, crying, "No, no. There are still four days—and they said that the old King died smiling, saying that he had kept his promise, so he *knew* you hadn't failed."

Marlo drew in his breath with a sudden harsh sound. "*They said*—who in the name of all devils were you listening to, child?"

There seemed to be no response from Huon and Trad said dully, "One of the Lords Regent—the one who wears a ruby ring."

"God in Heaven!" breathed the juggler, his voice shaking. "The Lord Gabriel—the worst of the lot!"

Huon had lifted his head.

"Four days," he muttered—so at least that much had entered his mind.

During their journeying Trad had managed to tell Huon privately all that he had overheard, but though the man had listened with strained attention the empty look had remained and nothing except his unreasoned determination to reach the City seemed to have any reality to him.

Now he stood up slowly, looking towards the City as if he was going to urge them onwards, but in a flash his face changed.

"Here?" he said in a strange questioning cry, and his hand went up to the back of his head. "*Here*?"

He was staring at a small open space in front of them, where new undergrowth had begun to cover broken and trampled ground. He took one or two faltering steps and then like a sleepwalker plunged his hand into a thick bush. When he withdrew it, a sword with its blade broken a few inches below the hilt was in it.

He gazed at it for a moment, then with a shuddering cry dropped it and began a staggering run forward.

"What is it *now*?"

It was almost a shriek from Marlo and Trad, himself terrified, gasped out, "He has a fearful wound on his head—it must have happened here and he has remembered——"

He went running after Huon, trying to speak to him or stop him, and after a moment Marlo, having stooped to pick up the broken sword, joined him. But they could do nothing with the frantic man. Brushing them off unseeingly he plunged onwards, sometimes crawling on his hands and knees, sometimes stumbling at a desperate walk.

Not until they were within sight of a tiny church and a cluster of little cottages did Marlo, his face green with fear, use force. In the shelter of a small coppice beside a rough track he deliberately tripped the staggering figure, and as it crashed down he first broke the fall with his own body and then wrapped both his own and Huon's cloaks tightly around the fallen man, preventing movement. At first Huon struggled a little but then he lay still, his face turning gray and his mouth falling open.

"He's dying," whispered Trad in horror.

"Nonsense." Marlo, sweating freely, managed a reassuring smile. "He needs rest and quiet. And water. The skin is empty—I was making for a spring." He raised his head and looked around. He bit his lip doubtfully, then shrugged his shoulders. "You must go for water to one of those houses. Take the flask."

He bent again over Huon, rubbing his hands and then pulling up his tunic to rub over his heart.

Without a word, far beyond tears, Trad took the old leather bottle from Huon's wallet and ran out on to the track towards the cottages.

The first one he came to was obviously empty, the door broken down and the small garden rank with years of untended growth. He had run past it with no more than a single glance, thinking only that there could be no help there, when a suddenly blinding flash of knowledge brought him to a dead stop.

Just as he had recognized the City on the mountain, so he knew this little cottage. He glanced up and saw above him almost the same view of the City, glanced back and knew that it was in that small garden, then gay and sweet with flowers, that his memory of being held by loving parents was set.

His lips opened.

"Mother," he whispered, and then, "*Father*!"

For the first time he could remember their faces, both of them gay and young, his mother's sweet and pretty beneath curls as black as his own were dyed now, and his father's fine-featured and proud under the forward-swept corn-gold hair.

Then they were blotted out by Huon's face, gray and deathly through the white hair and beard, and he thought again only of his errand.

He ran as fast as his bare feet could take him on the rough track to the next cottage, trim and well-cared-for, and knocked hard on the low door.

If it had sprung open as he knocked it would hardly have seemed quick enough to his need, but in fact he was not kept waiting long. An old woman, with a kind simple face, opened the door and when he gasped, "Please—may I have a little water? My grandfather has been taken faint," she opened the door wider at once, clucking concern.

"Of course, of course, my dear child. Come in while I get it for you—cold from my lovely deep well."

This was obviously no countrywoman but someone accustomed to being asked for help and giving it. She made him sit down while she drew the water and then, in spite of his protests, gave him a mug of rich milk to drink while she fussed from cupboard to cupboard in search of a very special cordial that her brother, the late priest of the parish, had strongly recommended for the ailing old. She was just proposing coming with him to administer it to his grandfather and he was wondering how he could prevent her, when there was a peremptory knock on the door.

"Dear me, dear me," she cried, her face bright with pleasure, "*two* visitors in one day, and this usually such a quiet place—" and she hurried to open the door again.

"Good morning, madam. Do you remember me?" said a smooth quiet voice, and for a moment the world went black around Trad. Grandfather—*Grandfather*?

When at last he could see again Grandfather was actually in the room, while the old lady bobbed delighted curtsies at him. Almost without thinking Trad slipped off the stool, made a little curtsy and sat down again, burying his face in the mug of milk.

Through his eyelashes he saw Grandfather give a quick glance and then ignore him.

"Yes indeed, indeed, sir," the old lady was babbling, "how could I forget you? So kind you were when you came for the little boy—ah, the poor little dear, father and mother gone at one blow! But a kind grandfather to look after him—how is the little darling, still the breathing image of his dear young father? Such a *handsome* young man, with his lute and his golden hair and his laughter—alas for him and your lovely daughter!"

A rather sickly smile was curving Grandfather's thin cruel mouth, and his eyes were hooded like a vulture's.

"As you say, madam—still the image of his father. And, as you can guess, the light and joy of my life. I have left him in good hands that I might come to see you on his behalf—I know how fond you were of him. I was delayed on the way—" for a very brief instant his benevolent expression vanished. A snarl twisted his face and his unhooded eyes blazed with hate and anger. Trad remembered with a tremor the Lord Regent's reference to two weeks in his dungeons, and another terrified peep showed him that his grandfather's face was thin and worn, while he moved with a clumsy limp and kept one hand hidden in his robe. He must have been tortured to get the truth about the ring from him—Trad shuddered. He could not—*he could not* feel sorry for Grandfather even now and although it was *his* fault that this had happened to him, since he had found the ring and not told Grandfather.

The old man had recovered himself very quickly.

"Forgive me, madam," he murmured. "I was delayed by an injury and it still pains me a little. I have come to ask—it is the question of an inheritance—if you remember the child's father wearing a narrow gold ring? A small ring, perhaps on his little finger."

The old lady pursed her lips, solemn and important.

"Now let me see. A ring." Then she shook her head. "No, I am quite sure he did not. As he used to set out on his journeys he would comfort your daughter—poor little dear, she would weep to see him go, though how else could they live and he a minstrel?—by saying laughing—how he always laughed, to be sure—'I have nothing worth stealing except my lute. My lute is my fortune, and that I guard with my life.' No, I can see his hands now as I nursed him in that last illness, long and thin and bare and always moving, as if they searched for his beloved lute."

"The lute!"

Grandfather was standing as if struck to stone.

"Why, to be sure," cried the old lady brightly, "you took it with you when you took the little boy."

"The lute," said Grandfather again, hoarsely, and turned as if he would rush out at once. He recollected himself and turned back to thank her.

"Why, it's such a pleasure to hear about the dear little boy again," she declared. "And if it's a question of an inheritance would it not be well to search their house? No one has lived in it since they died. People say—" her voice sank a little "—that sounds of lute-playing are heard there at night."

"Superstitious nonsense," said Grandfather angrily and she agreed, though doubtfully.

He was nearly through the door when she exclaimed with a self-reproachful cluck, "There now, and I never asked you—I suppose he never reached you? No, no, I can't hope it with that dreadful wound in the head, but I grieve so for him, so set he was on finding the little boy, but in his state I doubt he got further than the foot of the mountain."

Trad sat frozen on his stool while Grandfather turned back slowly from the door. It was obvious that he was controlling a fury of impatience only by the strongest effort.

"Madam," he said gratingly, "would you begin at the beginning and tell me what you are talking about?"

In spite of his restraint the old lady looked frightened.

"Why, sir," she whispered falteringly, "he came—it must be now four months ago—asking for your son-in-law. He wept when he heard of his death, but when I told him of the dear little boy you had taken to look after he laughed a great laugh, saying, 'At last! At last I can fulfill my promise, and return!' Then he looked up at the City and laughed again, saying, 'All those years and right under their noses! Ah, if I could have known that man, what friends we would have been! But his child shall be mine, to guard and serve.' And with that he was gone."

"All this," said Grandfather, still with that terrifying restraint, "with a wound in his head?"

"No, no." The old lady was still flustered but she had talked herself out of her first fright. "That was—let me see now—two, or was it three—no, it was two days later. I heard a sound in the late evening and thinking Job's pigs had got into my garden again I went out and there he was, his head split open from crown to neck, covered with blood, stripped of all his bright armor and so near death that I do not know now how he did not die that night—and even less how he had dragged himself back to me. Job helped me carry him in and I nursed him for near three months. Three times he nearly died as the fever blazed up, and his wits were clean gone, poor soul, he remembered naught, so I thought. But one day I came back from Mass and he was gone, leaving only a note saying, 'I must go and look for him.' So I suppose he remembered about your little boy and set off to find him. And the wound barely healed and himself as weak as a child—or rather as an old man, for so he looked, his golden hair as white as snow."

Trad was rigid with agony—was there *nothing* she was not going to tell Grandfather?

"But there," finished the old lady with a sigh and a tear, "he cannot have gone more than a few miles, though indeed I have looked for him in vain as far as I can walk. Dead in a ditch in his pride and strength, I fear, yet gentle and courteous as he was, and full of pity——"

She might have gone on rambling indefinitely but Grandfather cut her short.

"Very sad," he said coldly. "But he certainly never reached me, nor do I know who he could have been. Thank you, madam, for your kindness. I will make a quick search through the house my daughter lived in and then return to my darling boy."

His lip lifted in an uncontrollable snarl as he spoke, and the old woman gazed after him doubtfully.

Trad slid off his stool again as the door closed.

"I didn't like him," he said in a gasp. "I don't think he would be kind to my grandfather. May I go out of the back door?"

The old lady was still so perturbed that she did not fuss him or even press the cordial on him as he seized his bottle of water—lying in full view on the table, suppose Grandfather had recognized it?—and with a quick murmur of thanks crept quietly out of the back door. Bending low behind bushes and tall grass he hurried as well as he could back to the coppice.

Huon was sitting up now, his face less gray but his eyes vague and wandering.

"You have taken your time," said Marlo crossly, snatching the bottle to put it to Huon's lips.

"Marlo." Trad was shaking so violently that he could hardly whisper. He could hear Grandfather's limping footsteps on the track. "Hide him. Cover him with the cloaks——"

With a quick glance at him Marlo obeyed, and they all crouched low, hidden by the dull-colored cloaks while the old man passed by, stumbling on the rough ground and muttering. "The ring. Then the boy. The ring. Then the boy."

"Merciful heavens!" breathed Marlo, when all sound had died away. "Who was that?"

Trad slipped in a little heap to the ground.

"My grandfather," he said between chattering teeth, and fainted.

Chapter Eight

HE came around in Huon's arms, with Huon's bearded face bending over him, still ghastly white but with full intelligence in its grave concern.

"Lie still, child," he said. "And drink."

He held the bottle to Trad's mouth, but the boy pushed it away.

"I had milk—in there," he whispered and shuddered as he remembered what else had been in there. Then he sat up quickly.

"Huon!" he said urgently. "I know a lot more now—" he broke off, suddenly remembering Marlo and looking around quickly for him. The juggler was standing a little way from them, watching them with his face curiously blank.

Huon looked around too.

"You can say it in front of him," he said gently. "He will not betray us. Though I think he will not help us further."

Unexpectedly the fat man's face went as red as fire and then instantly as white as it had been red.

"I dare not," he burst out, "and God's Body, don't trust me not to betray you! If they—if they—all I can do for you now is leave you, you will be safer so if they have come to know of us. You must do the best you can —what has a timid man like me to do with such as you?" Something like a smile twisted his face as if he was trying to show that this was only a joke, but he was trembling uncontrollably.

Trad gazed at him silently. He understood now how far Huon had meant that they could trust this man—as far as his courage went. But he, who had spent six years in paralyzing terror of his grandfather, would never in all his life feel scorn for a coward. He glanced up at Huon, fearing a little to see contempt or condemnation there, but the bearded face was gentle and understanding.

Shifting the boy on to one arm, Huon felt in his wallet and held out a handful of coins.

"Take them," said the deep friendly voice. "It costs money to hide."

Marlo stared at them both and then at the money. "And you?" he muttered.

"We," said Trad, sitting up straight and proud, but not without a practical thought of the two coins in his dress, "are protected."

The juggler's eyes opened wide. There was obviously a struggle in his mind, and then he took a quick step forward, almost snatched the money and made off at a quick pace without looking back.

Trad rolled off Huon's arm and stood up unsteadily, then stumbled after the juggler, who heard him coming and turned around, his face set and hard.

"Marlo," said Trad shakily, fumbling in his purse and getting out the coin there. "This is for Jokey. And Marlo—" his voice sank to a whisper "—don't mind. I'm frightened too. Only I've got to look after him because my father's dead."

The fat man's face was a study, flushing and paling in an agony of indecision and fear.

"I dare not, I dare not," he stammered at last, "but—listen, child, if you go forward, keep to that cleft—do you see it? And if you get to the houses—" he hesitated and at last muttered almost inaudibly "—ask for the house of Emias the smith." Then he turned and ran as fast as he could out of sight.

Trad could hear Jokey whimpering and was almost sure there was a despairing bark from him as he was carried away.

"I didn't even say good-bye to him," he realized, and stood for a moment struggling with tears before he went slowly back to Huon, who was sitting with his head in his hands.

"Not everyone can be brave, can they, Huon?" said Trad wistfully, sitting down beside him.

"Few, in such danger," said Huon, raising his face and showing it desperately worn and ravaged. "Child, if there is a friend in that house, go there for shelter. I—cannot go further today."

Trad turned to him indignantly and then saw with a shock of dismay that Huon was more than tired, he was right at the end of his strength. He had used the last of it to try to arrange protection for the child and now he fell back and lay still.

Trad thought again that he was dying. He half got up to run for help to the priest's sister, and then thought how dangerous that was. If *anyone* came to ask her questions she would tell them everything, and she knew too much about Huon. No, they must stay where they were. He must keep the sick man as warm as he could, and hope that he would be better in the morning. Stifling a sob, he collected the cloaks and wrapped them around the still form, then crept into his usual position curled against Huon's side.

"Never fear, little cousin." Huon's gray lips hardly moved but the deep voice, though faint, was firm. "What must be done can be done," and then with a short sigh he turned his head and sank into what seemed more like unconsciousness than sleep.

It was less the repeated assurance than those words —"little cousin"—which sent Trad's heart leaping towards hope again. Somewhere behind that barrier Huon did *know,* then—knew that Trad's father, with "his lute and his golden hair and his laughter," was his own cousin, the laughing lord who had been sent twelve years before to find him with the half of a ring, and whom he himself had been seeking, surely in order to get that ring. There had been no time since the terrifying encounter with Grandfather in the old lady's cottage for Trad to think out what he had said, but now it came to him slowly that Grandfather thought the ring was concealed somewhere in the lute. With another leap Trad remembered how the ring he had hidden had clicked home around the gilt rosette—*did the rosette itself conceal the second half of the ring?* His father's half?

Moving cautiously he slid the lute off Huon's shoulder and ran his fingers around the slightly raised circle. He wondered whether to use the point of his dagger to dig it out, and then decided against it. Suppose he could not put it back? There was no other hiding place so secure, and the possession of the ring alone would put them in deadly danger, even if they were not recognized. Then as he thought of that danger his heart sank again, and he cried himself to sleep, one hand clutching Huon's tunic and the other holding the soft silkiness of his toy Jokey against his cheek.

The next two days taught Trad, as deeply as a ten-year-old child could experience it, what the words which had so fascinated him, "the great and terrible quest," really meant.

Though Huon woke at first light and got somehow to his feet, his first few steps showed that he could not be allowed to leave the comparative shelter of the coppice and remote village until he was stronger. Trad argued and pleaded, soothed the man's agitation with calculations of the time there was left and the short time it would take now actually to reach the City, and even used his small strength to drag him back, not once but forty or fifty times during the day. It was the first time he had had to take over a period the full responsibility of decision, and the burden of it exhausted him even more than the physical effort of the day.

At times when Huon had accepted the necessity for rest and had fallen into the light doze from which he would soon wake up, gasping about the urgent need to move forward, the boy sat watchfully beside him and—to take his mind from the disheartening difficulties and dangers still ahead of them—thought seriously of the result of the quest. Starting with simple daydreams of all that could be done for friends like the Wise Woman when Huon became King, he began to understand how much more was involved.

Child as he was the journey through the countryside even in the comparatively easy conditions of full summer, together with all he had learned from Huon and Marlo, had shown him how deep was the sickness which destroyed the happiness of the kingdom. Huon and Marlo had told him that the impassable gulf between rich and poor, shocking though it was, was general through Christendom, but here in this land greater wrongs could be seen.

As long as the poor were protected in their few rights and possessions by the Law or custom of the land, administered with more or less justice and mercy by the King and his lords, they could be content enough plodding through their lives in the humble hope of reward in Paradise, helping each other from both fellow-feeling and Christian teaching. But in a land where the Law had become nothing but the will of a few greedy wicked men there was no protection for anyone. Nothing was safe, neither their lives nor their goods, and so every man thought of himself only. Those with power used it to get themselves whatever they wanted, and Diamond with his out-and-out robbers was hardly worse than any lord or knight throughout the land: those without power became cunning and selfish in defense of whatever they could grab or keep for themselves; only a few rare spirits or those taught by desperate danger stretched out a hand to those in need.

"Huon will put it all right," thought Trad eagerly, and then as time passed emptily, began to consider how.

He soon saw that it would not all be done as if by magic the moment Huon—somehow—entered the Gate of the City. The people might proclaim and crown the grandson of old King Tancred, but the Lords Regent were not likely to give up instantly the power which had been theirs for twenty years. There might be open war and even if not, Huon would probably have to fight some of them and punish others.

Sadly and anxiously Trad looked at the broken man he was guarding. Huon might say that what must be done could be done, but *could* anyone so seriously damaged do all that the King must do? Trad could not bear the thought of his trying to fight anyone with that wound still unhealed in his head.

"If I was a little older I could help him," he told himself, seeing himself as helpless for at least four years—three years? Surely at thirteen he would be old enough to go fighting? Then he realized how much this was still the daydreaming of his lonely upbringing—*of course* he and Huon couldn't do this singlehanded, even if he too became a champion of champions.

"There are those two country lords in the Forest," he suddenly remembered, and with a quickening of hope, "the Wise Woman said there were '*a-many*' who were against the Lords Regent. Perhaps they will follow the King—" somehow even in the secrecy of his own mind he felt it unwise to use the name Manfred "—if he gives them a leader. And when I am *older,* I can help too."

He began to plan to travel to the Great Forest as soon as possible to ask for help, but he was interrupted by one of Huon's attempts to get traveling again at once, and by the time he had got him quiet he and the man were both so exhausted that he knew he must ask for some sort of help *now.* As he carefully unpicked with the point of his dagger the stitches which held one of the silver coins, he was working out a story to tell, and as he knocked at the door of the same little cottage he had it all ready.

The old lady was delighted, though surprised, to see him again. She sat him down to another mug of milk and asked with a genuine concern about his grandfather.

Trad raised large tear-filled eyes.

"He is tired. We have been resting all today, and I have come to ask if I may buy some of your cordial and some food?"

He held out the heavy silver coin, but she hardly noticed, she was already planning to get Job from next door to help the old man indoors so that he could be properly nursed.

Trad was ready for this. He explained tearfully that his grandfather hated women, that when he was unwell it threw him into a dangerous fever if he even saw one.

"You see, my mother disappointed him terribly by running away to marry my father and he can't get over it," he finished rather uncertainly. He had discovered, to his surprise, that he disliked telling lies to the kind old lady, so he had substituted this, so near the truth, for a romantic tale he had prepared about disappointment in love. He was a little afraid it was *too* near the truth, but as the old lady shook her head, clucking disapprovingly but seeming to accept the story without surprise, he remembered that she believed Grandfather to be a kind and loving parent and grandparent.

She bustled about putting up a cheese pie and a large loaf into a packet for him, and looked for a flask for the cordial. Again he offered the coin, and this time she peered at it, exclaiming in astonishment at its value and asking how such a child came to possess it.

"A—an aunt sewed it into my dress for me for when we really needed it," he said anxiously. "Can't you take it?"

"Much too much," she said with unusual firmness. "Bless you, child, what I've done for you is nothing. And—" she swooped on him and kissed him, taking him by surprise "—you're such a *dear* little girl, you remind me so strangely of a little boy I once knew, a child whom everyone loved as soon as they saw him."

"Not everyone," thought Trad grimly, remembering

Grandfather and his friends, but the direction of her thoughts alarmed him.

"I never had a brother," he said hastily and then, partly to change the subject, deliberately laid the money on her table.

"Madam," he said gravely, "I beg you to take the coin. It is little enough to pay for what you have done not only for us but for that poor man and the young man and his wife you spoke of yesterday and, I doubt not, many and many more." Unconsciously he was speaking as he had heard Huon speak, and still without realizing it he bowed to her as Huon had bowed to the Wise Woman. Then, seeing her quite speechless, he gently kissed her hand, took the packet of food and the cordial and slipped quietly out.

"I will come back after and thank her properly," he promised himself, running quickly back to the coppice with the fear that Huon might have somehow managed to start out on his own, but the sick man was lying as he had left him, in a daze of exhaustion.

Somehow he got some of the cordial down his throat. It must, he thought, have been very like the Wise Woman's cordial, for it had much the same effect. After a little while Huon opened his eyes, murmured, "The weather is breaking," and with a heavy sigh turned his head and sank into a deep natural sleep.

He slept without moving until morning and then woke with his mind clear and some return of physical strength. But he had been right about the weather. Trad had been trying through the night to protect them from the showers which had started soon after dark. He had dragged branches to make a shelter and covered it with grass and leaves as the rain grew heavier. He had kept them fairly dry, but by daylight the rain had settled down to a heavy drenching downpour, and as they huddled beneath the cloaks to eat a hurried meal before setting out, Trad could not help wondering whether he had been wrong to prevent Huon going the day before, when the weather had still been fine.

As they struggled up through the rocky slippery cleft Marlo had shown him, splashing through suddenly swollen streams, hampered by thin greasy mud and horribly uncomfortable and clumsy in their sodden clothes, he became despondently sure that he had made the wrong decision. Yet Huon, though himself today, was obviously still desperately weary. He stopped more often to rest and went on again more slowly each time. The struggle became a nightmare which Trad never willingly remembered afterwards, a nightmare which tested to the utmost not only physical endurance but courage and determination. Under the heavy clouds and unceasing rain it was gloomy to the point of darkness in the cleft and as he fought their way upwards, trying to find the least difficult paths, anxiously nursing Huon's failing strength and at the end actually tugging and pulling the exhausted man up the last steep rise, the Wise Woman's words were beating in his mind—"Darkness and danger and maybe death"—and he could not feel the protection of the power with which she had comforted him.

It made things worse that they could not see the

City towards which they climbed, and as they came out of the cleft he looked eagerly upwards—only to find that they had arrived at the foot of a precipice. On this side of the City the mountain did not rise only in steep terraces, as it did where the main road climbed upwards, it sprang sheer almost up to the walls, and beyond the walls only the top of the great white Tower on the crest of the mountain could be seen.

"We can never get up that," thought Trad dully, and looked hopelessly around.

He felt a little better when he saw that a rough narrow track led to the right around the foot of the precipice. Bracing himself, he turned to Huon with the smile of cheerful readiness he had managed to show him all the time.

"It's better walking now," he said consolingly. "Can you manage?"

The white-haired man, half-collapsed against a rock, straightened himself painfully and looked around.

Then came one of the startling returns of strength he seemed to be able to manage in emergency—"Was this an emergency?" wondered Trad, puzzled. Erect and vigorous he stood, looking first upwards, then from side to side, like a soldier considering a position of danger, or perhaps someone looking for something remembered from far back.

"The track, Huon," said Trad urgently, terrified that he might suggest climbing the cliff above them.

"No." Huon spoke with absent-minded decision. "It will be guarded. The bushes have grown up so—ah!"

It was a small sharp sound of triumph. He swung

around to their right and plunged strongly through the soaking bushes.

Trad followed him, feeling rather sulky—*more* of this awful going? And who would be guarding such a track in such weather? A dripping branch smacked him viciously across the face and he stood still for a moment, screwing up his eyes to keep the tears back.

"Now, now."

Huon must have swung around instantly and come back to him. A comforting arm was around his shoulders, and the deep voice with a strange undercurrent of laughter murmured above his head, "Tears now from *this* champion of champions? Come, brave heart—it is not much longer."

Trad gave a rather wobbly smile, licked a couple of tears which had squeezed between his eyelids and said defiantly, "I'm not crying—I can go on forever."

Huon laughed, but with deliberate quietness, and taking the child's hand he showed him the deep narrow bed of a small stream, almost covered by the thickly growing ferns, which ran in the same direction as the track but gave them a path not much rougher and quite secret.

How important this was they learned less than an hour later. Trad first heard the heavy footfalls above them, but Huon was nearly as quick. Before Trad could grab his sleeve in warning he had gathered the child into a semicave made by the overhanging track and they crouched there, listening.

Above them another set of footsteps sounded, coming from the opposite direction.

"*No one,* in weather like this!" said a grumbling voice, sounding so near that Trad, who had been wriggling a little to avoid a runnel of water emptying itself straight down his neck, froze into unbreathing stillness.

"What, not for a kingdom?" answered someone in jeering protest.

The first man grunted.

"Not for *twenty* kingdoms would anyone climb that cliff. Waste of time!"

His companion laughed without answering otherwise and then they separated, the footsteps dying away in opposite directions.

It was some time before Huon gave the signal to go on, and then they crept with careful silence. They heard no more of the men above them, though, and soon the little stream curved away from the track and the crevice it ran in became so narrow that they had to wade, Trad knee-deep, in the center of the stream, and in places Huon had to turn sideways to get his broad shoulders through. Then abruptly the stream disappeared into a tunnel cut in a large rock which closed the crevice.

"The tunnel leads straight into an alley," said Huon in a noiseless whisper.

"In the City?" asked Trad hopefully. It was not really cold but his teeth were chattering and he was tired out holding his heavy soaked skirt out of the water—he had tried letting it drop, thinking that it couldn't be any wetter, and it had at once tripped him up.

"No, no, not to be as easy as that."

There was no laughter in the voice now and Trad could see that the new-found strength was nearly at an end. Then the man deliberately gathered what he had left.

"We must go through that," he said steadily. "Give me your hand, child, and fear naught. We are indeed protected."

"Yes, because otherwise one of those men would have seen us as we came out of the cleft," thought Trad instantly, and with renewed courage he took Huon's hand and followed him into the tunnel.

It was a horrible journey even for the boy. Pitch dark, with water high enough to go swirling around his waist and tug him strongly off balance, the tunnel seemed to go on forever. There were places where he had to duck his head and one where the water actually met the roof, and only a sharp command from Huon to hold his breath kept him from opening his mouth in a gasp of surprise which would have filled his lungs with water. Yet all the time the cold strong fingers that held his never loosened their clasp, though what was difficult for Trad must have been difficult to the point of impossibility for the very tall broad man, and once or twice he heard a stifled groan from in front.

"We are protected, we are protected," said Trad to himself, trying not to think of Huon falling or perhaps crashing his injured head on the rough roof, and indeed neither of these things happened.

After what seemed like a year in the darkness there was a glimmer of light ahead and the water suddenly became shallow as the stream rushed away through a deep drain to their left. There were bars across the light, and Trad was wondering vaguely why when Huon took his hand gently away and Trad could hear from his sobbing breaths that he was trying to do something which needed all his strength. Then there was a great clatter of metal and Huon's shoulders, which had been blocking out the light, disappeared.

Trad, who was so tired that his mind was working very slowly, realized at last that the tunnel had been blocked by a grating, which Huon had displaced so that they could climb out. One more effort and they were both outside, in the gray light of an overcast evening in a narrow alley stinking with filth and piled high with refuse. Huon was on his knees, trying to replace the grating, and Trad stooped at once to help him. Together they just managed it and then Huon went slowly forward on to his face and lay still.

Feeling numbly that this was going back to the very first time he had seen Huon, Trad struggled until he had got the man's face clear of the dirt. He had been giving small doses of the old lady's cordial through the day but there was still a little left at the bottom of the flask, which he had carried in the front of his dress. Some got spilled because of the difficulty of getting Huon to swallow in his awkward position, but after a few minutes the man stirred, lifted himself a little, and crawled into a sitting position against the wall.

It was obvious, though, that he could do no more, and Trad knelt beside him, begging him in a trembling voice to finish the cordial.

Huon opened his eyes. He could not speak, but he raised one wavering hand and just touched the boy's mouth.

Trad guessed that he meant that he should drink the cordial himself and after a moment of doubt he did so. There were only a couple of mouthfuls but the effect was amazing. He gasped as what felt like liquid fire went down his throat and into his stomach and almost at once warm blood started flowing through his veins until even his dead toes and fingers glowed with life. He could think again now, and he realized that he would have to leave Huon here and himself go to look for the house Marlo had whispered about. If he could not find it or if there was after all no help there—he shrugged his shoulders. He would come back and at least they would be no worse off.

After a moment's thought he slipped off Huon's shoulder the leather wallet in which the man had been protecting the lute, preferring their food to get wet rather than the precious instrument. And it was more precious than Huon knew—if he left it someone might steal it from beside the helpless man or, even worse, kill him in order to take it. So putting the wallet over his own shoulder he set off through the narrow stinking alleys of what Marlo had told him was the slums of the City, banished from inside the walls and yet huddling close to them for protection, and swallowing up what had been large houses and estates belonging to the lords, who had moved out in disgust when the riffraff came to their doors.

Although it was not yet dark and the rain had

stopped, there seemed to be nobody about to ask for the house of Emias, and he was just beginning to work out why, when he heard behind him down one of the wider alleys the stumbling clop-clop of an over-ridden horse.

He turned instinctively—and found himself looking at his grandfather, drooping in the saddle of a gray horse in the last stage of exhaustion. At the same instant Grandfather raised his head and looked at him.

Whether the old man actually recognized him or whether it was the lute, showing above the top of the wallet, which gave him away Trad was never to know. Without pausing even for thought the boy had gathered up his skirts and turned to run faster than he would have believed possible a moment before. He heard Grandfather's strangled cry, "*Trad*!" and ran even faster.

As he ran, though, he was making up his mind. His ears, alert for every sound, told him that Grandfather had hurled himself from the saddle and was coming after him on foot, his limp hardly hindering him. He would turn the next corner and then stop dead. He did not remember fetching out his dagger but there it was in his hand, and he reckoned quite coldly that it was long enough to stab through the throat of an old man who would not be expecting such a sting from a child he despised.

A man stepped out from a side alley in front of him and there was a shriek of triumph from Grandfather. "Tawny! Hold him!"

Trad came to a frantic stop, skidding a little on the

filth under his bare feet. He could not hope to kill *two* men——

But Tawny was not looking at him, his eyes were fixed straight past him. He raised his great bow, there was a sharp twang and an arrow zinged past the boy's ear—*and Tawny never missed*——

Trad whipped around. Grandfather, his hands at his throat, was staggering towards him. Then quite slowly he fell on his knees, from there face downwards to the ground and so lay still.

Without a glance at Trad Tawny ran past him, stooped as he went to pick up the arrow which had gone right through the old man's neck and lay free beyond him, and on to the far end of the alley. A moment later Trad heard the clatter of hoofs as the archer swung the tired gray around and ran with it out of sight.

Trad was left alone with the body of his grandfather. He stared at it, trying to make himself go near enough to be sure he was really dead, when there was a small bark, a scrabble of a single paw at his legs, and a little dog flung himself upwards into his arms.

Chapter Nine

NOTHING was ever to convince Trad so surely that they were protected as the arrival at this moment of all moments of a friend—of two friends, for as Jokey wriggled upwards to lick his face in an ecstasy of welcome, Marlo seized him by the shoulders.

"Child—*child,*" he said, and in the gathering darkness Trad did not guess at the tears in his eyes. "I have been looking for you since yesterday evening. Where is—Huon?"

Trad did notice the little hesitation before the name and thought he understood it.

"I had to leave him when I came to look for the house you said." His voice shook so that he could hardly get it out. "And then Grandfather chased me."

It was Marlo who dropped on his knees by Grandfather's body and said briskly after a very brief look, "Quite dead. Fortunate. I hope you can find the way back?"

His coolness had steadied Trad and he set off at

once. He had taken very special care, because towns were still so new to him that he dreaded losing himself in one, to notice something to remember at each corner he turned, and he found his way back without hesitation.

The alley had been a good hiding place, for the piles of refuse at the entrance had hidden Huon from any casual passer-by, and even the patrols who had swept the streets bare might have missed him. He seemed to be unconscious, but Marlo, with a quick uncontrollable look over his shoulder, knelt beside him and said in a low firm voice, "My lord, you must make one more effort—we must get you off the streets and you are too heavy to carry."

So Marlo too knew not only who Huon was but that he could always do what he must, thought Trad, as Huon opened his eyes and took Marlo's hand to help himself up. It took Trad as well actually to get him on his feet, but once there he walked steadily where Marlo led him.

They had in fact to go less far than Trad had walked looking for someone to direct him. There was a little two-story house leaning up against one of the great derelict mansions which had become a rabbit warren of a settlement for those strong enough to fight their way into superior shelter; the little house had a smithy occupying most of the ground floor, and a large loft-like room above. Marlo took them through the smithy, nodding to a very large grimy man who was blowing the bellows of the fire, and with a doubtful glance at Huon showed him the steep ladder which led upwards.

He also looked around the smithy, as if wondering whether it was safe enough to leave him down there, but when he looked back Huon had taken hold of the narrow rungs and was pulling himself doggedly up the ladder.

Marlo followed him as quickly as possible, and by the time Trad had worked out a way of climbing without putting Jokey down, Huon was lying flat on a long pallet with Marlo kneeling beside him again.

"—to rest as long as possible. You may trust the boy to me," he was saying, his voice strangely pleading.

Huon turned his head and gave the juggler a slow smile of absolute friendship and confidence, then closed his eyes and went to sleep.

Marlo drew a long unsteady breath and stood up.

"You are both soaked to the skin," he said practically. "Help me to get him undressed—no, no, we shan't wake him, with any luck he will sleep for the next two days."

"Two days?" said Trad in alarm, trying to work it out. It seemed years since he had told Huon they still had four days, and surely two days from now would be too late—

Marlo was looking at him rather oddly.

"Don't think," he said grimly, "that you will live to have more than one try. So it might as well be the last possible moment, since that will at least give—him—time to gather the strength he will need then as never before or after in his life."

Trad could see the sense in this and he moved forward to help strip Huon of his sodden clothes. As he did so, something Marlo had said registered at last. He stood still, his eyes startled.

"When did you know I was a boy?" he blurted out.

Marlo, already more than halfway through the job, laughed with friendly mockery.

"After all the beastly little urchins I have taught to dance I am not likely to mistake a boy for a girl."

He wrapped the naked man in ragged but surprisingly clean blankets, and then produced another to put around Trad when he had got out of his dress and equally wet ragged breeches and shirt. By then the sense of safety had let Trad feel how tired he was, and though he sat down to a bowl of soup he fell asleep over it, and did not feel Marlo lay him gently down on a pile of straw in the corner.

He slept through until late the next morning, and Huon was still asleep when he woke. The girl's dress was there, smoky and crumpled from having been hung by the smithy fire, but dry and warm, and he got dressed. Marlo was out but he came back just in time to stop Trad climbing down to the smithy to make friends with the big dark man.

"You must stay up here," he said urgently. "*No one* must see you. And though Emias is safe he can say nothing to you—he is dumb."

The juggler's laughter-creased face darkened, though it was later that he explained that Emias, his younger brother, had had his tongue torn out years ago on the orders of a lord who thought the young smith not respectful enough. Now he just repeated his warning that Trad must not be seen, since the patrols of the Lords Regent rode unceasingly through the streets and alleys and searched any house they chose to consider a possible hiding place. When at last Huon and Trad had to go out there were various precautions which would be taken, but that would not be until the last night.

"There is a late moon," finished Marlo with satisfaction.

"But then they'll see us on the road," objected Trad.

Marlo gave him that rather odd look again.

"You will never get up the road. Tell me, did you hear—him—say that he had climbed up the *outside* of the Tower?"

"Yes." Trad spoke eagerly and proudly. "He said before once that he had been up the Tower and seen the King, but I didn't know he had gone up *outside*—" he paused, visualizing that heaven-touching Tower, and then understood what was in Marlo's mind.

"You mean up that—awful—cliff?" he asked unbelievingly.

"You will not get to the City any other way," said Marlo flatly.

Trad sighed. This was one of the things that could be done because it must, he supposed rather gloomily.

Marlo was watching him.

"You must go, surely," he said without expression.

Trad realized how deliberately Marlo was avoiding asking questions and how little he actually knew, whatever he guessed.

"Would you rather not know? Would it be safer for you?" he asked bluntly.

The juggler gave a sharp unamused laugh.

"Who could suppose a timid man like me would give up all thoughts of safety for the sake of—what? A little copper coin and a little boy who said he was frightened—too," he mocked himself.

Thinking it out rather doubtfully, Trad saw at least that Marlo had already done enough to cost him his life if he was discovered—to know more would not put him in any more danger.

He sat down confidingly against the man's legs.

"May I tell you?" he said, and began his story.

It took a long time to tell because he kept almost nothing back, and he remembered bits which later excitements had put out of his mind. Marlo heard him out in total silence, looking from time to time at the deeply sleeping man on the long pallet. At the end Trad, who had stopped only for a meal of bread and cheese, gave a sigh of relief.

"So you see, Marlo, he will be just the sort of King you wanted," he said earnestly, and then his voice wobbled, "if only he isn't too badly damaged to do all the fighting he'll have to. Will there be people to help him?"

Marlo went on looking down at him for what seemed an extraordinarily long time. Then he looked at Huon and back again at Trad.

"Have you thought—" he began, and then stopped suddenly. "Perhaps better not," he muttered. "And after all he *will* have to do the fighting—" he looked up as if he had decided something. "Yes, there will be people to help him," he said slowly. "The Archbishop has been kept almost as a prisoner in his Palace because he has opposed the Lords Regent—he must come out to crown the King, and he will bring the Church to his side. And the people will be for him—which is more than nothing when they have a leader at last and someone to love——"

"And the lords and knights who have been turned out or hurt by the Lords Regent," broke in Trad eagerly. "I know some, they're friends of mine——"

"I don't doubt it," said Marlo, smiling a little. "And as for that injury—" his face became very serious and troubled. Then he bit his lip. "There is a Healer—a good one—in the Bishop's old Palace just now. I could—" he paused "—I could go to fetch him." He stood up abruptly. "I will go at once," he said in a hard voice, and was gone.

Trad too had stood up, gazing after him. He had just seen something very clearly. Marlo had been shaking like an aspen leaf, he was afraid to his soul of going out, he was afraid every moment these dangerous guests were under his roof—but he had gone out to look for them, he had brought them here, and he had gone out again to get help for Huon.

"I have seen the bravest man I have ever known," thought Trad soberly, and turned instinctively to Huon to share his new knowledge with him.

But Huon slept on. He did not even wake when the

Healer brought back by Marlo within the hour handled and examined him.

The Healer, a man with a quiet face and the most beautiful hands Trad had ever seen—except perhaps Huon's—had stood back in astonishment when he first looked at the sleeping man.

"But—I know this man. He is a Healer—a true Healer, not one of those false ones who cheat the trusting poor—what has happened to him?"

Marlo, who was still shivering slightly, said with emphasis, "I have heard that all that House have something of the Healer in their hands. Look at the back of his head—and tell us whether he will be fit for the burden which must be his at least for some years."

It was obvious that the Healer understood what he meant. He bent over Huon, carrying out a complete examination gently and carefully. Then he sat down and asked Trad the fullest possible questions about how the injury had happened and the effect it had had since.

Trad, who did not need to be told that this man was to be trusted, answered with everything he knew, and at the end the Healer sat silently for a time, his head bent. Then he looked up slowly and spoke, surprisingly, to Trad and not to Marlo.

"The wound has healed—ask me not how. There are miracles which even Healers do not understand. The weakness now comes, I think, from the mind. While his memory is held from him the gap between what he knows he must do and what he knows about it destroys the healthy balance between mind and body, and the agony of the mind is reflected in the exhaustion of the body."

Thinking back, Trad could see that this was true.

"Do you mean," he asked with new hopefulness, "that when the key unlocks his memory he will be well and strong again?"

"I see no reason to doubt it," said the Healer with quiet certainty. "Though—that is a fearful wound. He may for some years suffer from the disabling headaches he must be having now." He turned quickly to Marlo. "Let him sleep as long as he may—he heals himself. When it is time for him to wake, give him this potion. It should keep the headache back at least until he has done what must be done."

He stood up, bowed—again surprisingly—to Trad, and went quietly out.

"Well," said Marlo with a fat chuckle of satisfaction. Trad turned to him.

"We owe all to you," he said quietly. "I shall not forget—he will not forget—you will always be our friend, won't you?"

It was evident that Marlo was deeply moved, though after his nature he tried to cover it with a joke.

"It would be something indeed if I could be Juggler to the Royal House," he laughed.

"Of *course,* if that's what you want," said Trad, laughing too. "Is the Royal House the same as the Royal Family? Will you tell me about them? I know hardly anything."

"And should know all," murmured Marlo, and for the rest of the day told the boy the ancient stories of the Kingdom and its kings, explaining among other things what the Lord Regent had called "the ritual nonsense" of the King's Week. The first ruler, another Tancred, had entered the Gate between the hours of sunset and sunrise with only one follower and taken the City by a startling piece of bluff. Himself only the younger son of a poor Norman baron, he had created for himself the Kingdom of Taschia, and his descendants had held it ever since, with the heir traditionally claiming the Kingdom by presenting himself at the Gate of the City between sunset and sunrise within a week of the last King's death.

Not all of the Kings had been admirable, but around all of them had been that bright aura of unaccountable power, and their hold over the imagination of the whole Kingdom explained why the Lords Regent had never dared to do away with the old King.

Trad, listening enthralled, interrupted only once. A tale of murder had suddenly reminded him of Grandfather's still body, and he came out with a question which had been puzzling him ever since he had got away.

"Marlo, *why* did Grandfather guard me like gold and do anything to get me back?"

"I think there is no doubt," said Marlo slowly and carefully, "that as he stood over your dead father he recognized him. He meant—" he hesitated "—he meant, I am sure, to claim your inheritance and rule it for you. Having reduced you, as he thought, to a mindless slave."

Trad thought about that.

"But if he had been *nice* to me, he could have been sure I would do anything he wanted," he argued.

"How would such as he think of that?" said Marlo scornfully. Then thoughtfully, "And indeed it isn't even true. Did your mother do *everything* he wanted? The wicked can only bind people to them by fear." He laughed aloud. "To try to bind one of *your* House so!"

Trad hugged his knees joyfully. Because he knew he had been afraid of Grandfather he would never think himself very brave, but at least he *had* got away, he was not totally unworthy to be a cousin of such a House.

"Go on," he commanded, and Marlo obediently went on telling of the glorious youth and manhood of the old King who had just died.

The quiet day had the strange effect of making the boy feel more tired than ever. He did not realize that this was the tiredness of the long time of strain making itself felt as he relaxed, but he lay down thankfully as soon as Marlo suggested bed, and when in the morning Marlo warned him that since he must be awake and active all the night he must rest as much as possible and sleep if he could, he tried his best to do so.

But thoughts of the night made him more and more restless, and at midday, when he got up for a meal, the juggler made no attempt to send him back to bed but began to tell him, as if he had a right to know, the details of the arrangements he had made for the night.

To get them out of the house unnoticed, a large empty house about a quarter of a mile away was going to be set on fire, and ahead of them down the track to the precipice a large drunken group was going to occupy the attention of the guards while Huon and Trad quietly slipped by.

"No one will be hurt," said Marlo rather quickly as he watched Trad's face.

Trad wondered doubtfully how he could be sure of that, but before he could ask Marlo had gone on briskly, "And I have a present for—our friend there. Emias is forging a new blade for the hilt he pulled out of the bush—I suppose it to have been his own, and at least he will need a sword."

Trad was delighted.

"May I pay Emias?" he asked eagerly. "I have some money——"

"Why no, we shall send in a heavy bill to the Palace in a week or so's time," jested Marlo. "And Emias can spend that week making a rather smaller sword—big enough, let us say, for a ten-year-old lord."

Trad drew a long breath of ecstasy.

"I *hope* I'm going to be a good fighter," he said, blurting out an anxiety which he had been feeling for some time. "*He* is a champion of champions and all the Kings you told me about were splendid with sword or lance."

"No reason why you shouldn't be." Marlo sounded comfortingly matter-of-fact. "Old King Tancred was undefeated in war and peace, and the renown of the High Prince Conrad both as swordsman and jouster rang through Christendom."

"Yes." But Trad was not quite satisfied. "Was the laughing lord renowned?" he asked rather wistfully.

Marlo's face changed. He had never been so passionately in earnest.

"Now, how could he be!" he exclaimed. "Never forget, my lord, what the Lord Hilarion gave up for—for the sake of his duty. Barely seventeen, almost at the beginning of life, he left his home and friends, ease and laughter and the chance of fame, to wander in secrecy and danger on a quest which must have often seemed hopeless and which took from him all the years of his young manhood. Heaven knows how the old King, repenting so late of his wicked folly, persuaded such a young man to such a task."

The boy, at first taken by surprise and delight at being addressed, for the first time in his life, as "my lord," had quickly become serious as he listened.

"Perhaps he was the sort of man who didn't need to be persuaded," he said slowly, thinking with sorrowful regret of the father he would never know as a person.

"Maybe, maybe," said the juggler, shrugging his shoulders lightly. "Maybe in the whole world there is after all *one* man who will not only give away his life but disinherit himself in doing it."

He saw Trad's puzzled face and said, deeply serious again, "Remember—he was the cousin of the King. If neither Conrad nor Conrad's son returned the Kingdom would have been his by right. That was why the Lords Regent did not watch him—what man could they imagine who would give away a Kingdom for some scruple of loyalty or impulse of chivalry?"

"I want to be that sort of man," said Trad softly.

"You have started the right way."

There was a note of dry amusement in Marlo's voice but Trad did not try to think this out. A terrible thought had struck him.

"Did Grandfather want to have Huon killed and then have me made King?" he whispered in horror.

"Certainly Huon had to be killed if your grandfather was to rule," said Marlo carefully. "But if you are now blaming your existence for the attack on Huon, that is nonsense. It was the Lords Regent who ordered his death—and they, we hope and pray, do not even know of you. He would have had to die even if you had never been born."

That made sense and the boy relaxed. He had kept his little dagger with him as he slept, and now he ripped open the stitches at his waistband and held out the second silver coin to Marlo.

"Please take it for the sword. We—we shan't want it for anything else."

Their eyes met but neither of them got nearer saying what the child knew as well as the man, that if the sword was not paid for now it might never be.

Marlo took the coin and looked at it curiously.

"Where did you get this, child?"

"The Lord Regent—the Lord Gabriel—gave it me." As Trad thought how the Lord Regent's silver was being used he began to giggle. "It's funny, isn't it? It's terribly f-funny—" he gasped, and then found that he could not stop laughing—if it *was* laughing while he shook all over and tears poured down his face.

The next moment he was on Marlo's lap, held comfortingly close to the big fat body which looked soft but in fact was solid and muscled and strong.

"Now, now," said Marlo soothingly, patting his back and stroking his hair, "now, now. Cry it out, my little one—you have been through too much."

The trouble was that Trad could not stop, and at last Marlo took him by the shoulders and held him away so that he could see his face.

"Hush, hush!" he said in a voice of comic alarm. "*He* will think I am beating you—and as we both know he would rise from the sleep of death to protect you. Has done so," he added in a very low voice.

Trad hiccuped, choked and at last got control of himself.

"What it must be," murmured Marlo whimsically, tossing the silver coin in the air, "to be one loved at sight by all men of goodwill."

This must be a joke, and the boy chuckled obligingly, though he felt bound to point out, "The Lord Regent didn't give it me because he loved me—it was to spy on Grandfather."

"I was not including the Lord Gabriel among the men of goodwill," said the juggler dryly, but Trad had gone on to other thoughts.

He slipped off Marlo's knee and stood very straight.

"I'm glad Grandfather's dead," he said firmly. "I'm glad it was Tawny who killed him. I'm only sorry it wasn't me."

Laughter shook the fat man all over.

"Good, good, good! I was beginning to wonder how the Kingdom would fare—angels may rule in Heaven, but on earth we need something tougher. Tears and pity and too many scruples are not for rulers."

Trad felt this was something he would have to ask Huon about, but Marlo had glanced out of the window at the position of the sun and now got up. Muttering something about the final arrangements, he looked dubiously at the sleeping man, and told Trad to wake him if he could, though without using force, before he came back. Then he swung himself quickly down the ladder.

Trad, having hastily scrubbed his face, knelt beside Huon.

"My lord my cousin," he said softly, thrilling to the words—and found Huon's blue eyes looking straight at him.

"Time to get up, child?" said the deep voice cheerfully, and the man sat straight up, moving easily and vigorously. Cautious because of what the Healer had said, Trad concentrated on telling of the practical plans Marlo had made.

"He thinks we can climb that precipice," he finished, his voice faltering a little.

"Ho, does he!" The flash of mischievous amusement

altered the grave face completely. "I'd like to see *him* do it."

"Can't we?" said Trad blankly, and Huon broke into one of his deep roars of mirth.

"Who said *we* couldn't? His plans are well enough, except——"

He was interrupted by Marlo's return. They heard his hurrying feet across the smithy floor and he missed his footing on the ladder once in his frantic haste. He was chalk-white and sweating as well as trembling with fear.

"The word has gone out—an old man and a little girl—how could they know?" He struck his hands together violently. "That archer——"

"It wasn't Tawny!" cried Trad fiercely. "He wouldn't, unless—" He stopped, thinking in horror of torture, and then in enormous relief remembered. "He never saw Huon, he *couldn't* have said about him," he said positively, and then as his mind worked like lightning, "It must have been Grandfather! He knew about Huon's white hair and him looking for me. He must have gone to Diamond for help when he couldn't find me, not knowing——"

"—that Diamond had sold himself to the Lord Regent," finished the juggler gloomily. "They are not fools—start thinking of an old man and a child and how can they help looking twice at the Master of music and his granddaughter? Now what do we do?"

He and Trad looked helplessly at each other. Then both started violently.

Huon was laughing, a deep sound of immense amusement.

They swung around to see him rubbing his hand over his thick white beard.

"It will be pleasant," he said gaily, "to be a young man again."

Chapter Ten

ONCE Huon had pointed the way the others were not slow to follow it.

"Wait! Wait!" said Marlo sharply and flung himself recklessly down the ladder, while Trad scurried to the wallet, gently removed the lute and rooted around for the Wise Woman's little wooden box. When the juggler came panting up with a heavy bundle which he deposited on Huon's bed, Trad thrust the open box at him, whispering urgently, "His hair was *golden* before."

It was no sort of explanation but Marlo surprisingly made the leap to understanding. He looked closely at the roots of Trad's hair—it was two days since he had rubbed any of the ointment in—and muttered, "So! I thought perhaps you took after your mother."

He turned rapidly to producing scissors and shaving tackle, but after he had hacked off the greater part of Huon's beard he left him patiently scraping away at the stubble and came back to Trad. From the bundle, which clanked as he burrowed in it, he took a new boy's suit in dark green, with long slim hose and a tight-fitting jerkin.

"Almost good enough for a little lord entering his City for the first time," he said jestingly.

"Did you buy it for me, Marlo?" whispered Trad, overcome.

"I will add it to the bill," Marlo assured him briskly, and giggling, Trad pulled off his girl's dress and swaggered into the new clothes.

He was looking down enchanted at his long green legs when Marlo touched his dark curls, shook his head a little and murmured, "Wine, perhaps."

A bottle of wine was fetched from a cupboard, and Trad's hair was soaked, rubbed, thoroughly toweled and rinsed in hot water Marlo brought up from the smithy.

"A-ah!" said Marlo in a long breath of satisfaction when he saw the result. He touched the front of the damp red-gold curls with fingers which shook a little, then quickly combed the hair forward as Trad had remembered his father's hair. He looked at the result, then abruptly brushed it back and found a hood—not matching the suit and rather large, but covering up all that bright hair.

"They will be looking for golden hair," he said in explanation, and then while Huon was still scraping his face Marlo rubbed the Wise Woman's ointment into the thick white hair—though touching very gingerly anywhere near that terrible wound—and combed it through until it was evenly dark all over. As if the sight of the wound had reminded him, he also gave

Huon the potion which the Healer had left for him. Huon, who appeared to be entirely preoccupied at the moment with his appearance, fastidiously feeling over his skin and shaving again any roughness, accepted it absently and drank it without comment.

"Huon," said Marlo—the use of that name surprised Trad until the juggler's careful choice of words made him realize that he too had understood the danger of reminding the man of his lost memory—"only by the precipice can the City be approached. Can you climb it?"

"I should hope so," said Huon casually, scowling horribly over a tricky bit by his ear. "I did it for a wager when I was young and a fool."

"Alone?"

The casualness of Marlo's tone matched Huon's, but he was taut with anxiety.

"No, with the son of another Lord Regent," muttered Huon and then with an extraordinarily youthful arrogance, "a soft ninny whom I had practically to carry up."

"A soft ninny?" Marlo laughed lightly. "The son of which Lord Regent would that be?"

"The Lord Gabriel."

Trad's hand flew to his mouth, and though Marlo's control was good his face went gray.

Huon swung around. It was obvious that—unlike other times—he was aware now of what he had just said.

"Ah," he said after a moment. "You think they may remember—they may be expecting us there." He was silent, his face becoming very grave and sad. "How we pay for our follies—how we pay," he murmured, and then made a little quiet gesture of resignation. "No matter. As you said, it is the only way. If I only had—" he stopped abruptly.

Marlo had gone down on one knee.

"Sir," he said, "deign to accept the best we have to offer—poor though it is, it comes with our love and duty."

Huon gave him a quick frowning look and turned to the bed. He unrolled first some leather clothes of the sort which in earlier days had been worn under armor, then a coat of mail—not a knight's, for it was heavy and clumsy.

Marlo was instantly there to help him put them on. They were not a bad fit, though a little short and very loose—Trad guessed that they might have belonged to Emias, who was not much shorter and a lot thicker than Huon.

"There is no helmet," said Marlo apologetically, "but there is—this."

He shook out the center bundle of rags and a bright sword lay flashing on the blankets.

He and Trad both looked eagerly but anxiously at Huon, hoping that he would be pleased, fearing that he would be too much reminded. Huon was looking only at the sword, his face unreadable. Then slowly he stretched out his right hand and took hold of the hilt.

Trad fancied that the sword leaped at his touch, fitting into his hand as if it belonged there, and he expected Huon to wave it in the air with some warlike gesture. But instead the man turned it very slowly downwards, and then with a quick movement thrust the point between two boards so that the sword was held upright with the cross of its hilt uppermost. As a continuation of the same movement Huon sank down to his knees, his eyes fixed on the cross, his face rapt and still.

Trad was holding his breath. He knew the customs of chivalry, such as the vigil before knighthood, only from the jeering remarks of Diamond and Grandfather, but they had always been part of his secret dream and now he quietly knelt beside Huon, folding his hands as he must have been taught in babyhood. Instantly one of the long beautiful hands encircled both of his, and though Huon did not look down at him and after a quick glance Trad too looked only at the cross, for that little time he was conscious of being part of Huon as Huon was part of him, and both of them giving themselves to the great and terrible quest which would be only just beginning when they entered the City Gate.

"Amen," said Huon quietly to that unspoken thought, and rose lithely to his feet. He pulled the sword out with a quick practiced flick and made as if to sheathe it.

"No sheath, but there is a belt," said Marlo in a low shaken voice, and fumbled to clasp it around the clumsy mail. Huon settled the sword through it, then suddenly spread out his arms in a huge exultant gesture.

Trad could not take his eyes from him.

This tall young black-haired man, whose face for the first time was not scored by the deep lines of pain which had aged him even more than the white hair and beard, would have been a faintly alarming stranger if it had not been for those moments of communion, but no change would ever make Huon a stranger now.

"Oh!" exclaimed Trad joyfully. "The Healer's cordial is even better than the Wise Woman's or the old lady's."

Huon turned towards him laughing, one eyebrow raised quizzically, but he did not ask for an explanation.

"Now, friend Marlo," he said with the easy authority of one born to leadership, "your plans are good, but—no revelers. Only enemies shall die tonight. Nor is there need. The fire, yes, that is well thought of—so we shall get unseen to our private road to our goal."

Marlo was very quick.

"Ah—I wondered how you reached here. I bought *my* passage with a joke and a trick—and a cracked rib," he said rather grimly.

"Oh Marlo!" Trad took his hand, looking at him with wide eyes. He thought of all Marlo had done, and all the time in pain. "I think you are the bravest person I know," he said gravely, and the juggler went slowly crimson, looking dumbly at Huon.

The young man looked back at him, unsmiling.

"He speaks for me," he said quietly. "You have done for us—more than I could have dared hope from anyone. We do not need now, I think, to ask any more from you. Except just to stop the revelers."

"I can send a message for that," muttered Marlo. "But—" then he seemed to decide to say no more at the moment.

Trad was not listening.

He had just realized that they would have to go back through the tunnel, crawling through the grating into darkness and stumbling through the water——

"Marlo." Huon's voice was strangely urgent. "Has it rained since we have been here?"

Marlo too was watching Trad, who was struggling with his feelings without any thought that they might be obvious to the others.

"Not a drop," said the juggler with emphatic cheerfulness. "Everything has dried up."

"There will be very little water in the tunnel," said Huon gently to Trad. "Hardly enough to get those fine new hose wet."

Trad nodded without speaking, not even able to smile.

It was the darkness rather than the water—but what must be done could be done, Huon said.

He turned quickly to repack the lute in the wallet.

"Well, you need not burden yourselves with *that,*" said Marlo practically. "Leave it here—I will guard it well——"

"No, no!" screamed Trad. "I must have it, I must have it! Or—" he stopped as it occurred to him that he could get the ring out now—both parts of the ring, if it was as he hoped—and give it to Huon. The ring might even be the key which would unlock Huon's memory.

But then it might on the other hand only bring on one of the desperate fits of trying to remember which destroyed his physical strength. Could that be risked at *this* time, with all his strength needed as never before?

He looked at Marlo as if he could help, and then remembered that although he had told him about the ring he had left out—not deliberately, but for some unconscious reason—the one fact that he had picked up the ring stolen from Huon and dropped by the Lord Regent, and had hidden it in the lute.

He himself would have to decide.

With his face twisted in agony he clasped the lute closer and sobbed, "I must have it, I must have it."

The eyes of the two men had met in perplexity and trouble. Naturally, they were connecting this outburst with the fear he had just shown, and they came simultaneously to the conclusion that his father's lute was a talisman to him, that he would feel braver with it.

"Take it, of course," said Marlo briskly at the same time as Huon said gently, "You shall have it, child. But you are right that it is better hidden. Pack it in the wallet. No need to take food—we shall eat before we leave."

He glanced at Marlo, who nodded.

"The moon rises soon after twelve. That will give you nearly four hours of light before sunrise—is that enough?"

"It will be enough," said Huon with a serenity new to him. "It would be unwise to start in the dark." He looked thoughtfully at Trad. "Can you sleep, child?"

Trad looked up from his task of fitting his little fur Jokey comfortably into the wallet with the lute.

"*Now*?" he asked, shocked, and Huon laughed, sat down on a stool and began to tell stories.

Marlo disappeared once to send the message to the "revelers" but returned to add his contribution to Trad's entertainment. He made them both weak with laughter by acting all the parts in a foreign wedding he had once attended, and then insisting on teaching the boy a very complicated back somersault with a twist in it because, he said, he wasn't wearing skirts any longer. When Trad finally collapsed, breathless with exertion and giggles, Huon said commandingly, "Enough, enough! The boy must sit still for a little." He then picked Trad up, settled him on his lap and began to sing, soft crooning songs which reminded the boy of some dim memory. He closed his eyes to think about it, and when he opened them the room was quite dark except for a glimmering rush light in the corner and a red glow from the window.

"Good," said Huon, grinning and stretching his arms as Trad sat up, startled. "We were just thinking of feeding you in your sleep. That—" he nodded at the window—"is Marlo's little fire. Eat your soup and we'll join the gaping bystanders."

It appeared that both Marlo and Emias were coming with them, Marlo to put back the grating so that no one would get the idea of following them, Emias—so Marlo said with an odd little smile—to guard his nervousness on the way back. It was also decided as Trad ate that since they would be moving away from the fire, Trad had better be asleep again to give them an excuse for hurrying "home."

So he was slung over Huon's shoulder, partly muffled in the cloak which also covered the mail, and the party set out.

The fire lit up streets far away from it and there was also a faint light from the rising moon, so that they had no difficulty in finding their way, nor were they challenged among the various hurrying groups. A few armed men could be seen, but they appeared more interested in the fire than in anything else. Their alley was deserted, and Emias kept guard at the entrance—Marlo muttering something to him before leaving him—while the others noiselessly removed the grating.

It was much less frightening than Trad had expected. Huon climbed in first and Marlo put Trad into his arms. There was only a trickle of water, and though the smell was abominable and the darkness as thick as before, the boy found himself thinking mainly how much warmer Huon's hand was this time and how much more easily he moved, and he was taken by surprise when they came out of the tunnel—it had seemed not much more than a few minutes.

The narrow overgrown crevice in which the stream ran was in darkness, though above the moon's light was strengthening minute by minute.

"No use trying to rush this," murmured Huon in Trad's ear, and they groped their way with extreme caution against noise, even though they could hear nothing from above. Trad's sharp ears, though, picked up some sounds from behind them and he tugged at Huon's hand to draw his attention to it. To his surprise he saw the dark head, dimly outlined against the light above, shake quickly and a brief gleam of moonlight through a gap in the ferns showed him that Huon was smiling a little. Puzzling about this, Trad crept on, feeling in front of him for loose stones or sudden cracks. There were leather soles to his green hose, and though at first they had felt uncomfortable to one who had never in his memory worn shoes, they certainly made things easier on this rough going. All the same it was a slow business and Trad glanced up sometimes at the moon, watching with dismay the rapid pace at which it climbed the sky. But at last they came to a stretch he thought he recognized as the place they had come down into the crevice, and with a quickening heart he moved a little faster, only to bump into Huon, who had come to an abrupt stop.

A man's voice, startlingly loud, suddenly broke the stillness.

"Well, my lord, no one and nothing. I told you we should have been on the main road. You and I and five of my best men wasted here——"

"*Diamond,*" thought Trad, feeling cold all over, and it was certainly the Lord Regent who answered him in cold anger.

"You take him for a fool—I warned you not to underrate that Family. I tell you he will come here, and at the last moment—and the cliff can be climbed. If he met that other before you killed him—if you killed him——"

Trad saw Huon, black in front of him, tilt his head up at the sky, nod, and then bend down. The next moment the deep murmur said, almost as if inside his head, "*Stay here,* child. If I do not come back to fetch you, Marlo will take you to the Great Forest, to the Wise Woman," and then Huon was gone.

Listening with all his might Trad guessed that he had drawn himself out of the crack and was making his way through the bushes so that it would appear that he had come down the track and the crevice would remain undiscovered—the child's mouth set like steel. Go on living when Huon was dead and the Kingdom in the unchallenged power of the Lords Regent?

With less skill than the man but just as noiselessly because he was so small and light, he climbed out and wriggled towards the track.

He was still in the thick of the bushes when he saw Huon appear on the top of a high cluster of rocks at the far side of the track, his drawn sword in his hand. Without pause he leaped down, and through the startled shouts Trad heard the clang of two rapid blows and two separate screams of pain.

Sure that no one would have any attention to spare, Trad broke from the bushes and ran for the same cluster of rocks. Almost before he had started to run he had decided agonizingly that there was nothing he could do to help—*yet*—and so he did not show himself, he crouched behind a rock and peered through a crack, every muscle tense and his little dagger in his hand.

He saw that Huon had gone right through the group of armed men and turned to face them with the wall of the cliff at his back. The moonlight shone full on him and Diamond, whom Trad had immediately picked out swore in a soft explosion.

"By-our-Lady, the ghost after all! Send him back to hell where he belongs——"

One man lay still on the ground and another leaned up against a rock, coughing and coughing while a stream of something dark came from his mouth, but Diamond led the others in a rush—five men fully armed, with shields and helmets, against one in ill-fitting mail with his head bare and no shield.

Trad, dazzled, saw Huon's face grow bright with terrible laughter. With a great shout of "Ha Rollo!"—that battle cry of his Norman ancestors which had burned across Christendom—he leaped towards his attackers, brought his sword across Diamond's helmet with a force which threw the man helplessly into a huddled heap five yards away, reversed his stroke and split another man's face from eyebrow to chin, and then, light on his feet as a cat, regained his defensive position while the three men left fell back a little.

"Archers, archers, I *said* we needed archers!" It was a scream of rage from the Lord Regent, easily picked out by his gilded crest. "Where are they?"

"Supposed to be coming, they were following us," growled one of the men bitterly. He was eyeing the tall laughing figure with grudging respect and before he had finished speaking he had leaped forward, as if to take him off guard.

His blow, aimed low, met only Huon's sword and the return thrust left his shield arm hanging limply. The Lord Regent and the other soldier instinctively closed in on either side, and for a few moments there was a confused mass of movement, the quickly repeated clang of sword on sword, or sword on plate armor, and the stamp of mailed feet on rock.

Then a figure split away from the mass, reeling backwards to crash downwards at full length, and following him the whole whirling mass moved as Huon drove his two remaining opponents in front of him. The soldier tripped over his fallen friend and went headlong, obviously knocking himself out. Huon was left with the Lord Regent, an experienced fighter and no coward, who defended himself with all his advantage of armor.

"*Gabriel,*" said Huon softly, and laughed. "I think the Kingdom will be better without you!"

The heavily armored figure faltered and the face below the gilded helm suddenly showed ghastly in the moonlight.

"*You*—it is *you*—" choked the Lord Regent, and with a violent movement broke away, trying to pass Huon on his left, either in flight or to get the advantage of the ground. Huon laughed again, leaped three feet to his left, and his sword came down in a terrible blow which clove the gilded helm and the skull beneath it as if they had been made of butter.

The Lord Regent's body tottered, spun around and fell, nearly taking Huon with it because his sword was so firmly fixed in the split skull.

Trad's breath came out in a small shriek. Behind Huon Diamond had got to his feet and was staggering purposefully forward, the soldier who had been stunned by his fall was picking himself up, and the one whose face was a raw mask of blood had crept around almost to the cluster of rocks where Trad crouched, and was waiting to join in the attack of the other two.

Strangely, it was Diamond Trad fixed his mind on, not the nearer men. Huon was *not* going to be brought down again by a blow from behind—like an arrow from a master bowman the boy shot across the fifteen feet of space between them, straight for Diamond's legs. Diamond, his eyes glaring at the back of his old enemy, never even saw the child until the small furious charge tripped him from his uncertain balance.

With a skill borrowed from Marlo Trad rolled himself from under the falling body, then flung himself on top of it and drove his dagger as hard as he could through the elbow joint of the armor on the man's sword arm.

At the same moment a small black-and-white fury hurled itself at Diamond's leg and fastened needle-sharp teeth on the place behind the knee where for a walking soldier there was nothing but leather. Looking up amazed, Trad saw Jokey's master launch himself from the very top of the cluster of rocks on to the soldier with the split face, springing high into the air and driving his feet into the back of the man's neck as he came down. Both men crashed to the ground as Huon swung around and met with bare hands the attack of the third soldier. The single sword rose but Huon caught the man's wrist above his head and Trad heard the bone of the arm snap. Then Huon, with a roar like a lion, seized the soldier around the waist, lifted him high in the air as if he were no heavier than Trad, and smashed him against the nearest rock, where he hung limply for a moment before sliding to the ground.

A ten-year-old boy with his attention distracted and a little dog with only three legs were no match for a fighter like Diamond. Cursing in a soft continuous snarl he rolled himself to his feet, and though his sword arm hung useless he caught his sword in his left hand, knocked Trad over with a sweep of his arm and made at a limping run for the track to the town.

Huon started after him, then stopped to snatch up a sword lying ownerless on the ground. As he did so Diamond turned and threw his sword like a knife. Huon sprang aside but the tip of the blade caught him across one eyebrow and the spurting blood blinded him for long enough to let Diamond disappear among the bushes.

Holding the blood back with his sleeve, Huon started off again but was stopped by Marlo's sardonic voice. Raising himself on one arm the fat man called out, "And have you time, my lord, for a game of hide-and-seek?"

Huon cast one look at the sky and came back.

They saw the brightness fade from his face. In a dull voice he said, "He will ride to the City and they will cut us off at the top."

"Not ride," broke in Marlo. "I set the horses loose. And the dog lamed him—he will take time to get to his men. You still have a chance—are you not going to take it?"

Huon stared around him.

Among the litter of bodies, the man Marlo had jumped on was quite dead with a broken neck, and there was no one else alive enough to take action.

"Yes," he said, in the same dull voice and went over to Trad. "We must go, child."

Trad had only just got over being sick. When Diamond had swept him aside he had fallen on the wallet, badly bruising his side, and it had taken him a little time to discover that he had also broken the lute. He looked up rather stupidly and then suddenly saw things clearly.

"But you must have the ring, Huon," he gasped, fiercely pulling at the wood of the broken lute until he had the gold circle clear. It was—it *was* doubly thick now! "It's two—one was yours and one was my father's and you have to have both——"

But Huon was not listening.

His eyes had widened as he saw the ring, and now with a little cry he swept the loose hood back off the boy's head and stood looking at the strange silver lock gleaming among the gold, as it had gleamed betrayingly in the golden hair of a dead minstrel when an old wizard looked down at him, as men remembered it gleaming on the head of the High Prince Conrad and, as few living men could recall, it had gleamed in the hair of the last King Tancred, for whom this child had been named until his own baby tongue had given him his nickname.

Huon's deep voice pealed like thunder, his face blazed with light—

"Silver hidden in the gold—
Young man hidden in the old—
Laughing lord with weeping eyes
Bring King and ring before sunrise!"

Then he flung his head back and looked up at the sky-touching Tower which as a boy of seventeen he had, incredibly, climbed.

"Old man," he cried, "I too have kept my word!"

With one of his great laughs he swept Trad up on to his feet.

"Put on the ring, little cousin! We go to the City!"

Chapter Eleven

THE ring, made for a man's little finger, fitted quite tightly around the boy's slim thumb when Huon pushed it on but Trad, though thrilled and breathless, was a little bewildered. Was it because the ring might come off as Huon climbed if *he* wore it? Or was it for the laughing lord or his son to bring the ring back—he could not think it out, but one thing was clear in his whirling mind. He could not go without saying good-bye to Marlo, who by following them with Jokey had saved them again.

He ran across to him where he lay, propped on an elbow to watch them, and then saw the horrid angle at which the fat man's left leg lay sprawled.

Trad caught his breath as he realized.

"Huon!" he cried. "The archers are coming—they'll kill Marlo, he can't run away or hide! How can we go —*you said only enemies would die tonight.*"

Huon, gazing up at the moonlit cliff, swung around. With three long strides he was beside them, then on his knees to straighten the broken leg with strong gentle hands. His face was as agonized as Trad's.

Marlo, gray and sweating, managed a croak of laughter.

"The trouble with angels is that they may be *in the habit* of throwing away Kingdoms! Roll me into the ditch, my lords—I can play 'Dead dog' as well as Jester, and who will spare a sword thrust for a fat dead man when nobler quarry is just ahead of them?"

While he was still speaking Huon had sprung up and was already gathering him carefully into his arms. Exerting his great strength he lifted him quickly and laid him in a dry grass-choked hollow which might once have been a ditch. Without a second's pause he then undid his belt, pulled the mail shirt over his head and laid it gently over Marlo and Jokey, for the little dog had crawled down to him.

"It has served nobly but it is too heavy for what is left," he said, and then gravely bent his knee to the ground in the reverence paid to kings before turning to Trad.

"Up, child, your legs are not long enough for the climb," he said, stooping for the belt.

"On your back?"

The man paused while a thought altered his face.

"No, clinging at the front like a monkey—the belt will fasten you there, but you must hold as tightly as you can without strangling me," he said quickly and picked the child up facing him.

Puzzled but obedient, Trad wrapped his legs around Huon's waist and his arms around his neck, while the belt clasped them firmly together. He did not see how Huon could climb the cliff like this, and though he was quickly proved wrong as the man climbed steadily and fast, leaning well out from the rock instead of hugging himself to it, he still did not see why the back should not have been better.

It was not until they were more than halfway up and he was peering down over Huon's shoulder to see how far away the ground was, that he understood. Small below them two men were running—he had forgotten the coming archers, but Huon had not.

His arms tightened involuntarily. If Huon was killed —then he relaxed. If Huon was hit they would both fall, both be killed; Huon had only provided against arriving at the top with a dead child on his back.

"But even that wouldn't matter if *he* was alive," thought Trad, worried. "Perhaps if the arrow hit me it wouldn't go through to him——"

"Are they there?"

Huon's voice, though a little jerky as he pushed himself up from an awkward toehold, was cool and cheerful and Trad tried to answer in the same tone.

"Yes, but—" he giggled "—one of them has just fallen over the other. He's—he's *broken the other man's bow*. The other one's very angry. They're arguing——"

He stopped. The argument, very brief, was over and one of the manikins was positioning himself as far back as the ground allowed—stringing his bow—raising it——

"Is this the worst cliff you've ever climbed, Huon?" asked Trad in a high squeak.

An arrow smacked into the rock just above Huon's right hand as it crawled up searching for a handhold and the shaft stood quivering, forced deep into a crack. Coolly Huon's hand came around it, tested it for firmness, and used it as a handhold to haul himself up another two feet.

"Useful," he said approvingly. "No, no—in the Holy Land we fought a battle up and down a cliff worse than this."

"What were you doing in the Holy Land?"

Trad's mouth was so dry that he could hardly get the question out as the next arrow whizzed past his cheek and fell blunted from the rock behind him.

"Keep your head behind my shoulder," said the unhurried voice and Trad obediently shrank into himself. "I was in search of your father on a false trail. Misled by the old King's verse I was looking for a young man disguised as an old one—how was I to know it was a *prophecy*?" He gave a short not very amused laugh. "*Not* one of the usual gifts of our House," he mocked himself.

"*They*'re music and healing, aren't they?"

Trad knew he must keep the talk going. He controlled a shudder as an arrow whined just over his head and fell back from the rock—the side of the steel arrowhead even slightly scratched his ear as it rebounded.

"And a small gift for war," said Huon dryly. "The next King must have a little more than those—a care for both mercy and justice, a gentle heart and a tough mind. Don't you agree, cousin?"

He broke off as the next arrow actually went through his hair.

"This is good shooting," he said with a matter-of-factness which was oddly comforting, and then rather slowly, "but either not quite good enough or—perhaps—" the voice quickened to a sudden tension "*—the best I have ever known.*"

"Tawny!" shrieked Trad. As the next arrow smacked just by Huon's thigh he risked a peep over. They were too high now for him to be sure, but it *looked* like enough Tawny—and he had broken the other man's bow—*and Tawny never missed*—he exploded into delighted laughter.

"Careful, child—even with such a marksman accidents can happen," came Huon's quick warning, and then Trad felt a quick tremor of laughter go through him. "A friend of yours? Fortunate indeed for us that the Kingdom has become littered with your friends. Fortunate now and in the time to come. *Ah!*"

On the long breath he reached up over his head and in one pull drew himself and his burden up over the edge of the cliff on to the gently sloping yard of ground between it and the City wall. He rolled sideways at once, digging fingers and toes into the ground to save himself from sliding over the edge again, but Trad thought he had been hit and he cried out frantically.

"No, child, no." Huon was shaking and breathless from the effort of that last tremendous pull but his reassurance was warm and amused. "We must not give him, though, a target he could not be expected to miss." Fumbling a little he undid the belt. "On your belly, child, until we reach that rock. There we shall be hidden."

Trad reached up first to wipe away the sweat mixed with blood which was still trickling from the eyebrow into Huon's eyes and then obeyed, wriggling like a snake with his eyes firmly turned away from the two-hundred-foot drop on his right. When Huon told him it was safe he stood up, looking with some dismay at their way ahead. Nowhere was there more than three yards' ground at the foot of the wall, and in places it was broken away into deep cracks, black bottomless chasms in the moonlight.

"Quickly, little cousin."

The deep voice was unusually urgent as Huon stood holding his hand out, and Trad gave a startled look at the sky.

The moon still rode serenely overhead, but there in the east was an unmistakable lightening in the sky. Dawn was here—and sunrise could not be far off.

With a little sobbing gasp he seized the long hand and scrambled along the dizzy way.

They made good speed for a time but then the boy flagged. The buckle of the belt had pressed against his bruised side and as he ran the pain became so great that he did not know how to go on. Only Huon's hand kept him going, half lifting him over rough ground and carrying him completely over the cracks.

Then Huon paused, saying quickly, "It will be better now—we must leave the wall and get on to the road."

Blinking wearily Trad could see that the ground fell

away entirely here—cut away perhaps for safety in defense—and they would have to go down a steep slope to one of the ordered terraces which bordered the main road.

Huon's voice too was ragged with exhaustion, but he put an arm around the boy and swung him down the slope, then took his hand again for the run across to the main road, climbing steeply here in the last few hundred yards before the Gate.

Both of them heard at the same moment the distant beat of hoofs coming up the road from farther down the mountain.

"Run!" said Huon.

Trad took a step forward and the pain brought him to his knees.

"But you—don't need me—" he got the words out somehow as he snatched at the ring on his thumb, trying to pull it off, "—take this—it's you they want——"

He saw above him the quick loved flash of laughter.

"Child, don't you know *yet*?" gasped the deep voice as Huon swept him up into his arms and began to run, stumbling a little on the rough ground and then settling down to a steady pace as he reached the smooth leveled road.

The beat of hoofs was nearer—the horses must be laboring up the sharp rise nearly as much as the man was—but Huon had already—tears were pouring down Trad's face as he thought in dizzy snatches of that victory in appallingly uneven battle, the burdened climb—*how after all that could any man do this even if it must be done?*

"For the Kingdom," said a ghost of a sound above his head.

The blue eyes were nearly closed, the man was staggering as he pushed himself up the slope but somehow, unbelievably, he kept on as the sky brightened behind him and the horsemen beat their foaming horses nearer and nearer.

So it was that as, by the ancient tradition, the waiting trumpets were raised to signal the first glimpse of the sun's rim above the horizon and the hushed crowd massed behind them pressed forward in almost unbearable tension, the Lord Hilarion stumbled through the Gate of the City with his King in his arms.

Born in Buenos Aires, Margaret Lovett grew up in England and holds a History Honors Degree from St. Hugh's College, Oxford. After college, she bought a little cottage where she meant to live quietly and write, but World War II intervened, and she found herself with four London slum children sharing her home for a while. Later, she went into a branch of the Foreign Office where, when the work began to tail off, she discovered that she had enough time—"in the office"—to write the first of her several published books for young readers, *An Adventure for Fivepence.*

After the war she took on several jobs she describes as "really useful work" because of "a sense of guilt about the years I pursued my own occupations at the public expense." Finally, she settled into boys' preparatory school teaching which she enjoyed but felt to be rather limiting. Then, a different kind of teaching job materialized, in a school in Berkshire, England, for disabled boys of high intelligence, which Miss Lovett has found totally satisfying and absorbing. With the little time and energy her busy schedule there leaves, she continues writing—partly, she admits, to have something to read to a class of 12-year-olds.